THE SUICIDE SQUAD:
SHELLS FOR THE SUICIDE SQUAD
AND OTHER STORIES

SHELLS FOR THE SUICIDE SQUAD
AND OTHER STORIES

By Emile C. Tepperman

POPULAR PUBLICATIONS • 2022

PUBLISHING HISTORY

"Shells for the Suicide Squad" originally appeared in the June 1940 (Vol. 7, No. 1) issue of *Ace G-Man Stories* magazine. "Suicide Squad's Murder Lottery" originally appeared in the August 1940 (Vol. 7, No. 2) issue of *Ace G-Man Stories* magazine. "The Suicide Squad and the Murder Bund" originally appeared in the November 1940 (Vol. 7, No. 4) issue of *Ace G-Man Stories* magazine. Copyright 2022 by Argosy Communications, Inc. All rights reserved.

SHELLS FOR
THE SUICIDE SQUAD

CHAPTER 1
THE CHIEF GIVES
THE PASSWORD

ON THE seventh of April, 1940, Kerrigan and Murdoch and Klaw were in widely separated parts of the United States. Johnny Kerrigan was in Omaha, visiting his mother. Dan Murdoch was in Montpelier, Vermont, where he had been going horseback riding with a red-headed beauty by the name of Evangeline Mercer. And Stephen Klaw was trolling for swordfish off the coast of southern Florida.

The seventh was a Sunday, and it was the last day of a three-week vacation which had been forced on the three agents of the F.B.I. by their Chief.

Three weeks had been too much for that action-loving trio. They were, each and severally, becoming restless and impatient. Dan Murdoch had a faraway look in his eyes as he withdrew his arm from around the slender waist of his red-haired beauty; Johnny Kerrigan patted his mother's hair affectionately but absently when she asked him, with solicitude, whether anything was worrying him; and Stephen Klaw found suddenly that it didn't really matter whether he landed the giant swordfish at the end of his line.

1

They fired coolly, carefully,

so as not to hit a shell.

Kerrigan and Murdoch and Klaw were known as the Suicide Squad of the F.B.I. In action, they seemed always to be seeking Death. The more dangerous the assignment, the better they liked it. They had become spoiled for the normal, commonplace activities of ordinary people. And during these last three weeks they had been bored half to death.

So it was with a sense of relief and exhilaration that they boarded their respective planes for Washington, each thinking of the moment of reunion, when they would drink a toast out of Dan Murdoch's bottle of twenty-year-old Scotch—a toast to their next adventure.

And, unknown to them, their next adventure was already in the making.

The first inkling of it was vouchsafed to Stephen Klaw, whose plane was roaring through the night over the bleak flatlands of South Carolina, when the radio call came in.

There were eight passengers in the big airliner, and they were all busily munching the chicken sandwiches which the smiling hostess had served. Steve Klaw was the only one of them who noticed the sudden veering of the plane. It was no longer heading due north toward Washington, but had turned into the teeth of an east wind, toward the coast.

Steve frowned, wondering what emergency had compelled the pilot to change his course. He said nothing to the others, though, but continued to enjoy his sandwich. Then the buzzer sounded at the rear, and the flag went up, indicating that the hostess was wanted in the pilot's compartment.

She, too, had noticed the change of direction, and she went

forward with a worried frown. In a moment, she returned and stopped at Steve's seat.

"Mr. Klaw," she said, "would you mind stepping forward? Captain Kennecott would like to speak to you."

Steve raised his eyebrows, and complied.

When he entered the small compartment, which seemed to be filled with instruments, the pilot nodded. "Hello, Mr. Klaw. Take these."

He stripped the earphones from his head, and handed them to Steve. Klaw took them, with an inquiring look.

"I noticed you've changed direction, Kennecott," he said. "How come?"

Captain Kennecott jerked his thumb to the earphones. "Put them on, and you'll find out. Washington wants you."

STEVE SHRUGGED, slipped the frame over his head, and adjusted the earphones. Kennecott snapped a switch. Steve said, "Klaw talking."

"Steve, I've got a job for you and Johnny and Dan!" He recognized the voice of his Chief, the Director of the Federal Bureau of Investigation of the Department of Justice. "I've pulled strings here in Washington, and I got the chairman of the Federal Aviation Commission to okay the plane's change of direction. Instead of flying straight to Washington, your pilot will go east, and put you off in the city of Forge Valley. I've also ordered the pilots of Dan Murdoch's and Johnny Kerrigan's planes to change their course for Forge Valley."

Steve whistled. "Must be important."

"Important?" The Chief laughed harshly. "The safety of the

United States of America will rest in the hands of you three boys when you get to Forge Valley, Steve. And it's dangerous. So dangerous that I'm sending all three of you there, in the hope that one of you will survive to succeed. I've already contacted Dan and Johnny, and they volunteered for the job. Now you—"

"You don't have to ask," Steve said, his eyes glittering.

"That's what I expected, Steve. Now listen carefully, and memorize these instructions. When you arrive at Forge Valley, you will register at the Forge River Hotel. From there you will go to the Continental Café. You will go to the bar, and wait there. Order a bottle of Bisquit Dubouché brandy, and keep the bottle in front of you on the bar, so that the person who is to meet you will know you. That person is a young woman. She is an agent of the United States Counter-espionage Bureau, and she is in great danger. She will greet you as Captain Paul Trent, of the U.S. Army, and that is the identity you are to assume. From there on, you will let events take their course, following any lead she gives you. Dan and Johnny cannot reach Forge Valley until least forty minutes after you, but their orders are to take up stations outside the Continental Café, and await developments."

"I have it all," Steve said.

"Good. One thing more—this young lady who is to contact you will give you a password. I can't mention it over the air, but…. Do you remember the name of that twenty-year-old Scotch that Dan pulls out every once in a while?"

"Yes." Steve smiled. That was a clever selection of a password. Few people knew the name of that Scotch—Highland Sabre.

"She'll mention that as the password. And now, I'm signing

off. I'd like to have you repeat the instructions, but the pilot and co-pilot in your plane will be listening in."

"It's not necessary, sir," Steve said. "I've memorized the instructions. Can you tell me anything about the job? What's the objective?"

"I don't know a thing, Steve. I can only tell you that the ultimate purpose is to locate and arrest the head of the German Secret Service in this country—a chap who is known by half a dozen aliases, among them von Spegler."

"Von Spegler!" Klaw exclaimed. "I've heard the name!"

"We're acting blindly in this, Steve, at the request of the Counter-espionage Bureau. This girl who is to contact you phoned them from Forge Valley, and asked for immediate assistance. They can't send their own men, because there's reason to believe that von Spegler's organization has obtained the names and photographs of every important counter-espionage agent. Therefore, they called on us."

"I see!"

Stephen Klaw took off the earphones and returned them to the pilot. There was a chill look in his eyes. It was true that he had heard of von Spegler.

IT WAS this same Ulrich von Spegler who had been the head of the German secret agents in Czechoslovakia during the tense months before that country's seizure. Von Spegler had been in charge of the Gestapo headquarters at Prague. And it was there in Prague that Ulrich von Spegler had committed an outrage which had come to the ears of Stephen Klaw.

The Gestapo had captured a young Czech intelligence officer

by the name of Jan Srydlo. Von Spegler had taken Jan Srydlo down into the cellar of the Gestapo headquarters, and had beaten and tortured him for three days and three nights in an effort to discover the hiding place of certain of Jan's colleagues in the Czech intelligence service.

Jan had died at the end of the third night—without speaking. But the things which Ulrich von Spegler had done to him, down there in the soundproof cellar, would revolt and shock the most callous of human beings, even in the mere telling.

The story of those three days and three nights had come to Stephen Klaw after many months, in a roundabout way. Steve had never commented on it. But Johnny Kerrigan and Dan Murdoch knew what was in his mind. Because Jan Srydlo and Stephen Klaw had gone to college together in Virginia, and they had formed the unbeatable team which had won the intercollegiate fencing championship during their senior year.

So there was a reason why Steve's eyes became frosty-gray at the prospect of coming to grips with the German spy-master, Ulrich von Spegler. Previously, there had been vague rumors that von Spegler was now operating in the United States. But this was the first confirmation of them.

Stephen Klaw returned to his seat. He sat rigidly, staring out of the window, while the plane roared toward the city of Forge Valley....

CHAPTER 2
ONE AGAINST
THE STORM TROOPS

K LAW HAD been standing at the Continental Café Bar for thirty-five minutes, and nothing had happened. The bottle of Bisquit Dubouché brandy stood in front of him, and he had taken three drinks from it, but no one had accosted him. No one had even looked at him.

He was beginning to wonder if he had gotten his instructions correctly, when he saw the girl in the red evening dress coming toward him. He had noticed her before, sitting at a table close to the dance floor, with two foreign-looking men. Even at his first casual glance, he had not failed to note and appreciate her exquisite and fragile beauty. He had watched her in the mirror over the bar, which was separated from the café proper by a row of potted palms, placed at five-foot intervals.

In the mirror he saw the girl coming toward him hastily. There was a smile upon her lips, but in her eyes was an urgent fear. Behind her, the foreign-looking man with whom she had been dancing bent and whispered swiftly to the other man at the table, then started after the girl, with a frown upon his heavy face.

Klaw lifted his brandy glass and sipped the liquor, with his eyes studying those two men. The one who remained at the table was thin and vinegary, with hot dark eyes, and black hair slicked down with pomade. His right hand rested on the table, toying with a glass, but his left arm hung at his side. Klaw had the impression that that arm was withered, misshapen.

The other fellow, the one who was coming after the girl, was florid, heavy-set, powerfully built; his dun-colored hair was cut in a close pompadour in the prevalent Teutonic style. There was an air of ruthlessness about him. Every fiber of him exuded overbearing strength and will-to-mastery.

Yet, in that quick moment before the girl reached the bar, Klaw wondered which of those two would prove the most dangerous in combat—the big fellow, whose very appearance warned of steamroller tactics with no holds barred; or the little one at the table, with the withered arm and the eyes of a poised cobra. Steve wished he had a description of Ulrich von Spegler. Either of those two men might be he. Yet Steve doubted it. He doubted that he would have the good fortune to meet von Spegler so early in the game. The spymaster was far too clever to appear in public in this way. He was somewhere in America, posing under another name and identity, of course.

The girl in the red dress was at Steve's side then, and he had no more time to speculate upon the identity of von Spegler. For she put out both hands to grasp his.

"Paul!" she exclaimed, and in her voice he thought he detected just the faintest trace of tension. "I didn't see you until just this minute. Have you been here long?" As she spoke, she pressed something into his left hand. Then she swiftly let go, and threw both arms around his neck.

"Oh, Paul dear!" she cried. "It's so good to see you safe!" And she kissed him on the cheek.

With her lips close to his ear, her voice dropped to the merest whisper—a whisper fraught with desperate urgency: "The name of the whiskey is Highland Sabre. For God's sake, be careful. If they have the slightest suspicion, they'll kill us both on the spot. Remember, you're my brother, Captain Paul Trent, Adjutant to the Chief of the Ordnance Division. Put that thing I gave you in your pocket. You're supposed to have brought it. You want to sell—"

Her whisper faded down to nothing, as someone behind her said, "Ah, Miss Trent, then this is the brother whom you have been expecting?"

THE MAN with the close-cut pompadour had a slight, half-ironical smile on his florid face as he looked into Stephen Klaw's eyes over her shoulder. From the expression Klaw couldn't tell whether he had overheard anything of what the girl had whispered.

She drew in her breath sharply, and took her arms from around Steve's neck. Steve could see in her eyes that something had gone wrong. Perhaps she had counted on having more time to coach him. She had not thought, apparently, that the man would follow her so closely. Now, with the meager information she had given him, Steve would have to follow her lead blindly, feeling his way.

She smiled at the big man, put, a hand on Steve's sleeve. "Paul dear, I would like you to meet *Herr* Mueller. *Herr* Mueller, this is my brother, Captain Trent."

Herr Mueller bowed from the hips, but without taking his eyes from Stephen Klaw.

11

"It is indeed an honor!" he said, with a slight curl of the lip.

"Pleasure!" Steve said sourly.

Herr Mueller turned and nodded swiftly to the thin man with the withered arm. The latter rose and hurried out of the café, through the front door.

Mueller swung back to face Stephen Klaw. He was bigger than Steve, and he spoke with a certain air of condescension. "You are ready to—ah—do business with us, Captain Trent?"

Out of the corner of his eye, Steve was watching the girl, hoping for a cue. She nodded her head almost imperceptibly, and Steve said, "Yes, *Herr* Mueller. I'm ready."

"You have brought with you the—ah—object in question?"

"Yes. I have it with me."

"Let me see it, please!" Mueller extended a big hand, imperiously.

Steve fingered the object in his pocket, which the girl had given him. He hadn't had a chance to look at it. But he had a good idea of its nature. It was cylindrical in shape, about four inches long, and tapered to a point at one end. His fingers touched grooves along the length of it, and there were several places where parts had been cunningly joined together. It weighed at least half a pound. He drew it from his pocket and held it in the palm of his hand so that Mueller could see it.

His eyes narrowed as he, too, looked down at it. For it was a perfect modeled miniature of a big shell. It was made of bronze. His inspection was cut short. Mueller's hand jerked forward, and his fingers reached out for it.

12

"I will take charge of it," he said, with a note of subdued eagerness in his voice.

Steve threw a lightning glance at the girl, and saw her shaking her head in the negative. He closed his hand swiftly, just as Mueller was about to touch it.

"Sorry!" he said.

He didn't know what the play was about. Until he could learn his role in this drama, he would have to take his cues from the girl as they went along. And since he didn't know what else to say, he just said, "Sorry!"

Herr Mueller's face grew red. "You do not trust me?" he asked softly, dangerously.

"No," said Steve. "I do not trust you."

MUELLER CONTROLLED himself with an effort. His eyes were suddenly flecked with red.

"My dear Captain Trent," he said in a quietly ominous tone, "you do not realize, perhaps, that you are at my mercy. You are betraying your country. You cannot afford to attract attention to yourself. The mere possession of that shell model would be enough to place you before a court martial. I shall now take it from you, and you will do nothing to prevent me!"

Klaw smiled. "Not so fast, Mueller. What about yourself? If I should be caught here, with this shell, you too would be caught. After all, you are a spy."

It was Mueller's turn to smile. "I will never be caught here, my dear Captain Trent. I have taken precautions. There are twenty of my men in and around this building. *Herr* Venic, whom you just saw at my table, has already given the signal that you are here. Believe me, dear Captain, you will never be allowed to leave this place alive—unless you turn over that shell!"

"H'm!" said Steve. He looked at the girl. She shook her head in the negative, then spoke to the big German.

"There is no reason why you and Paul should fight like this, *Herr* Mueller. I'm sure my brother has no intention of defying you. It's merely that he wants to be sure of getting his money. I'm sure that if you would arrange for him to meet your chief, the Graf von Speg—"

She broke off at a sharp exclamation from Mueller. "Quiet! You must never mention that name!" He turned to Steve, "It is out of the question, Captain Trent. You cannot meet my superior. You must do your business with me. I will take the shell. I give you my word that I will return in one hour, with the money—fifty thousand dollars in American money—as I promised your sister, here."

"No," said Steve, suddenly understanding the situation. "I want the money now."

Mueller shook his head. "Impossible. You must know that it is not so much the shell we want, as—as…." He shrugged, "Well, you realize that we must make sure we are getting what we want, before we pay. I must take it to someone, first."

"To von Spegler?" Steve asked.

"What difference is it to you, as long as you get the money?"

"I haven't got the money yet," Steve reminded him.

Mueller stared at him for a full minute with cold, fishy eyes. Then he said, "You are a fool, Captain Trent. You do not understand with whom you deal."

He reached into his breast pocket and withdrew a colored handkerchief. He raised it in the air, then lowered it and thrust it back into his pocket.

That action must have been a signal of some sort, for immediately a half-dozen men detached themselves from the bar and moved over, closing in on them. At the same time, several others came in through the front door; the thin man with the withered arm was at their head. Unostentatiously they angled over toward the spot where Steve and the girl were standing with Mueller. Their hands were in their pockets, suggestively.

The little man with the withered arm did not remain with the others. He went over to the table he had occupied previously, and sat down.

The girl, standing next to Steve, uttered a gasp. He saw that she was looking toward the table where the thin man had seated himself.

"It's Venic!" she exclaimed. "He's come back!" She was speaking swiftly, for Steve's benefit. "Those men are Storm Troopers, brought over from Germany. "They'll kill us and take the shell—"

Herr Mueller interrupted her with a growl. His men were already close, and he felt supremely confident.

"The shell!" he said harshly. "Give it up now—or die!"

He reached to snatch it out of Steve's hand, just as the first of the thugs came up to his side, their faces hard....

Klaw smiled thinly—and let Mueller have one on the tip of the chin. He brought his fist up only a short distance, but the impact sounded like the crack of a golf club against a ball.

STEPHEN KLAW was so slim and wiry that, at first glance, he might have been mistaken for a kid just out of college. But his slimness was utterly and dangerously deceptive. It would have seemed unlikely that he could pack much power behind a punch. But that lean and wiry body of his was made of whip-cord and spring-steel. When he struck Mueller, the German's head snapped up, and his spine arched back against the bar. His hands splayed out on both sides of him, the fingers twitching spasmodically. A queer little grunt escaped from deep in his throat, and he slid laxly to the floor.

Without giving him a second glance, Steve swung back to face the thugs who were closing in. His hands slid into his pockets, and he faced them, smiling tightly.

That swift blow of his had caused a flurry of excitement to ripple through the Continental Café. The orchestra continued to play, because it was at the far end, and had noticed nothing. But people sitting at nearby tables and at the bar stared with suppressed gasps.

If Steve hadn't spoiled the play, no one would have noticed that compact group of husky men closing in on the lone man and woman at the bar. The technique of these Storm Troopers was simple but efficient. They would have wedged in, forming a tight circle around Klaw and the girl. Inside that circle *Herr* Mueller would have smashed a fist into Steve's face, while another of the thugs might have done the same for the girl.

Then, still in a tight wedge, they would have hustled the two unconscious people out of the café, before anyone realized what was happening. They would have hinted that the couple were drunk, and that they were friends. No one would have thought of interfering. Outside, a car would be waiting, and they would have been whisked away in a flash—and two more victims of Nazi espionage would have disappeared from the surface of the earth.

Stephen Klaw was familiar with the technique. He had heard enough stories of how it had operated in the old days in Germany, before the Nazis had come to power, and later how they had used the same methods in Austria and Czechoslovakia. They had not hesitated to use it in the United States. But, heretofore, they had confined such activities to the people of German extraction they wished to terrorize into joining their movements. This was the first time, as far as Steve knew, that they had tried it on American citizens. The matter of the shell, which he now had in his pocket, must be of paramount importance to warrant these high-handed, strong-arm tactics.

Klaw had spoiled the smooth functioning of their machine, by taking the initiative. That blow of his not only threw them off their pace, but stopped them short for a moment. The Nazi mind, being trained to unthinking obedience to orders, was incapable of functioning with the swift speed necessary for an emergency.

The Storm Troopers halted, gazing down at the inert figure of *Herr* Mueller, and feeling in their pockets for weapons. Then they raised their eyes, muttering and staring at Steve.

He backed to the bar, with the girl beside him. His hands came out of his pockets, each holding an automatic. He kept the guns low.

"All right," he said softly, smiling at the thugs. "Which one of you monkeys wants to start something?"

The thugs looked to each other for inspiration. They were slow-witted, and without intelligent leadership they were useless.

But there was one man in that room who was far from slow-witted. His voice came harshly in a swift order in German. Klaw did not take his eyes from the thugs facing him, but he guessed that it was the viperish little Venic who had issued the command. He did not understand German, but the girl at his side translated in a hurried whisper: *"He ordered them to shoot us down."*

THE PATRONS of the Continental Café began to realize that something more than a drunken brawl was taking place. Someone shouted, "Police! I'll get a cop!" and started running for the door. One of the Storm Troopers stationed there caught him by the arm, and brought a blackjack down across his head in a vicious blow. The man folded up quietly, and the Storm Trooper let him drop to the floor.

The thugs around Stephen Klaw pulled guns out of their pockets, spreading out for better aim.

Klaw was already in motion. He put one hand behind him, and vaulted up on the bar. He began to shoot with his right-hand automatic, while with his left hand he reached down and helped the girl up beside him, then he gave her a little push toward the space behind the bar.

"Get down there," he ordered, "and run for the back. Get out.

Two of my friends should be outside by this time. They'll take care of you!"

The girl, trained in dangerous work, needed no second order. It was doubtful even if she heard what Steve told her, for his voice was almost drowned by the blasting of guns, which thundered through the café, rising in a great crescendo of roaring cacophony to obliterate the sound of the orchestra, like the molten eruption of some seething volcano which rolls down the mountainside in a landslide of doom, to bury a laughing and care-free city beneath hot layers of lava.

She leaped down behind the bar, and ran, crouching, toward the door at the rear, whither the two bartenders had already fled.

Stephen Klaw swung his left-hand automatic to bear upon the Storm Troopers. Its flame-belching muzzle joined the other gun, and twin streaks of fire lanced out at the gunmen. They were spread out, taking shelter behind the potted palms, and shooting fast, in the hope of cutting him down by the very intensity and fury of a continuous barrage.

Klaw, on the other hand, fired sparingly and carefully, knowing that he would never have an opportunity to reload. He triggered only when he saw an arm or a leg of a head behind a potted palm or behind an up-ended table. And every time he fired, one of his opponents fell.

But the battle was hopelessly one-sided. No man could hope to prevail against such odds. And though Klaw stood coolly on the bar, never moving from the one spot, supremely disdainful of the lead which whipped the air around him, he knew that it was only a matter of seconds before a shot would bring him down.

Yet that tight smile was still upon his face, and he never flinched. It was this utter disdain of death which had caused Kerrigan and Murdoch and Klaw to be nicknamed 'The Suicide Squad.' No one of those three ever counted the odds, or asked for an even break. It was that quality about them which had built their legendary reputation in the dark and turgid byways of the underworld. And it was that same quality which now put a queer and puzzled look into the eyes of those husky Storm Troopers, imported from a foreign country to spread a reign of terror in America. At home, in their own land, they were used to seeing men and women cower before them in abject terror. They were used to running wild, unhampered by human mercy, in great mobs, and to hunting down lone and frightened fugitives whose souls had been trodden into the dust, and who had neither the skill nor the strength to defy them.

But this was different. Here was a man who seemed no more than a mere boy, standing in the open and trading shots with them, with a reckless abandon which it was not in their blood to understand.

THE ROOM clouded with smoke and the air thickened with the stench of cordite. Women's screams mingled with the many-toned thunder of a dozen guns. Panic spread in the café. Patrons scrambled to escape, tripping over one another in their blind frenzy.

Barely a minute had passed since Stephen Klaw sprang to the top of the bar. Yet in that span of sixty seconds was compressed the swift action of an hour.

Venic—he of the withered arm—had disappeared. But his

thugs remained, firing continuously at the slight figure with the two guns, who seemed never to miss. They were counting his shots, and they knew that in another second his guns would be empty. Then they could rush him. Helpless beneath their flailing blows, he would be beaten to a bloody pulp.

But they were due for a surprise—a tornado of swirling action which burst in through the front doors. Perhaps they thought it was actually a tornado. Perhaps they took it for some flame-ridden emissary of the devil, come to claim his own. Certain it is that many of them had no time to think at all before death struck them down. The others, those who had a chance to turn and look, saw only two men. One was big, blond, with the shoulders of a stevedore. The other was dark and slender, lithe and quick, like a striking cobra.

Shoulder to shoulder they came through that front door, with guns in their hands and tight, set smiles upon their lips, and a grim look in their eyes.

The two Storm Troopers guarding the door raised their guns to shoot, but two slugs sent them crashing backward, out of the way. And then Kerrigan and Murdoch, standing in the doorway, turned their guns on the thugs who were sniping at Klaw from behind the potted palms. Those gunmen had no protection from this direction, and they didn't know what to do.

It was one thing for a dozen of them to attack a single man, sniping at him from cover. But it was altogether different to have the tables turned. They couldn't face hot lead in the open. Half of those remaining on their feet went down under the first volley from Kerrigan and Murdoch. The rest screamed in panic and turned to flee. They barged into panic-stricken patrons, stumbled over tables and chairs, as they gave way to blind terror.

As Kerrigan and Murdoch came forward, Steve Klaw jumped down off the bar. Then the three of them spread out over the cluttered floor, overtaking the routed gunmen and tapping each behind the ear. One or two escaped. The rest were no longer a menace.

Kerrigan and Murdoch came over to Klaw.

"Hi, Shrimp!" said Dan Murdoch.

"Hi, Shrimp!" Johnny Kerrigan boomed, with a laugh, like thunder.

Klaw grinned. "Hi, Mopes," he said. "You got here just about in time. I'd have been all through in another ten seconds. I'm scramming now. There's a girl somewhere outside, that I've got to find. You guys calm these people down, and look around for a thin guy with a withered arm. Also, keep an eye on that bozo on the floor by the bar. He's *Herr* Mueller, one of the minor aces of this spy-ring."

"What about von Spegler?" Dan Murdoch asked.

Steve shook his head. "I don't think he's been here. I'm going to play the game out to the finish. I'm supposed to be a certain Captain Paul Trent, who's willing to sell out the U.S. I'll stick to that, and maybe they'll contact me again. When you get through here, meet me at the hotel. If I'm not there, I'll get a message to you."

"Take care of yourself, Shrimp," Johnny Kerrigan growled. "Don't get in any tight spots. Remember, we may not be around to pull you out, next time."

22

"Nuts to you, Mopes!" said Stephen Klaw, and hurried out toward the rear door, pushing his way through the excited crowd of patrons.

He found a short passageway at the back, and darted through it, inserting fresh clips in his automatics as he ran. At the back of the building there was a door which opened into a yard. As he came out into the night air, he heard a high-pitched chorus of sirens and police whistles from somewhere out front. The law was arriving.

He looked around swiftly in the dark for the girl. He could see nothing, no shadows, no hint of movement.

"Miss Trent!" he called out softly. "Where are you?" A slow tension, pregnant with anger, crept into his nerves. There was no answer. Steve Klaw began to loathe von Spegler at that moment.

CHAPTER 3
THE SEÑORITA HOLDS A GUN

TO THE east, across the Forge River, the sky was lurid, aglow with the reflection of a hundred open-hearth shops, where steel casings were being forged for the great guns and huge ammunition shells that this city was famous for. Here, on the West Side, were the spacious residences of the wealthy, and the night spots where they spent the generous earnings of a wartime boom. Over there, on the East Side of the river, loomed the great plants of the Langley Powder Works, the Forge River Firearms Company, the Forge River Shipbuilding Corporation, and a dozen other immense industrial enterprises.

And while those sprawling factories made arms and ammunition, and planes and ships, on a mass production basis, they experimented, at the same time, in the interests of the United States. By arrangement with the War and Navy Departments, no new development in war equipment was offered for sale to a foreign nation until something even better was perfected for the use of the U.S.

Thus, the almost magically effective bombsights which we use on our own fighting planes have never been sold to another government. Similarly, the latest-type shells for the great naval and land guns were being made in those plants under the strictest rules of secrecy, and not for sale. Anything else, the belligerent nations could come and buy and carry away in their own bottoms, provided they had the cash to lay on the line. But the cream of American inventiveness and ingenuity and research was always reserved for our own use. So we can always be sure that in the event of our being cajoled, bullied or insulted into a war, we shall enjoy such a superiority of equipment that no enemy nation can ever become a serious threat.

But it was these very secret products of our own fertile resourcefulness that foreign powers coveted. Therefore it was not strange that the city of Forge River should be honeycombed with foreign spies.

Stephen Klaw, standing in the dark courtyard, with the din and clamor of the Continental Café's frightened patrons throbbing behind him, knew that this organization of von Spegler's was perhaps the most dangerous of all those operating in the city. And he was worried for the safety of the girl. He was sure that she had succeeded in making her escape from the crowded room in which he had held Venic's thugs at bay. But had she actually reached the outside? It was possible that she had been stopped in the passageway by others of Venic's men, and carried off. He shuddered at the thought of that fragile and delicate beauty of hers being placed at the tender mercy of a man like von Spegler. He remembered vividly the story of poor Jan Srydlo's three days and three nights of torture. Von Spegler would not hesitate to do the same things to a girl.

Stephen Klaw moved farther out into the yard. He searched the darkness with his eyes. He dared not call loudly for her, for fear that one of the spies might hear. He had not learned her first name, and if he was to continue to pose as her brother, he must not be heard calling her "Miss Trent."

There was an alley at the back of the yard. He followed it, disregarding the chance that some of Venic's men might be lying in wait for him in the shadows. He came out into the next street, and saw nothing. There was a row of brownstone boarding houses on the opposite side, while his own side was occupied by two or three apartment buildings and a row of stores. The stores were all closed now. There were no pedestrians within sight.

A car swept around the corner. Klaw thrust his hands into his coat pockets as he saw that it was veering in toward the curb where he stood, and slowing down. He waited, motionless, for any sign of hostility. It was a town car, with a liveried chauffeur at the wheel. He could not see who was inside.

THE CAR drew to a stop directly in front of him. The chauffeur sat stiffly, woodenly, without turning his head. The door was opened from within. A woman leaned out, smiling.

She was a tall woman, with dark hair and tawny, feline eyes. Long, amethyst earrings hung from her earlobes, and there was a necklace about her white throat which scintillated under the light from the street lamp. She was wearing a short fur cape over a black evening dress.

"Won't you step in, Captain Trent?" she asked. Her throaty voice held the faintest hint of a Latin accent.

At the same time, her right hand came into view, holding a small, pearl-handled pistol with a barrel which was hardly three inches long. It looked like a vicious little weapon at close range, and she held it pointing straight at Steve's stomach.

Klaw had his hands on both the automatics in his pockets, with the fingers curled comfortably around the triggers. He could have shot her from where he stood, through the cloth of his pockets.

Instead he said, "Anyone as beautiful as you doesn't need a gun to back up her invitation."

She laughed huskily. "Thank you."

She drew back into the interior of the car to give him room to climb in, but she kept the pistol visible, with the squat muzzle trained on him unwaveringly.

Steve stepped into the car and seated himself next to her, on her right.

The chauffeur came around and closed the door. Then he returned to the wheel. The sliding window at his back was open, and the woman said, "Go on, Basil."

Basil nodded. He shifted into gear, and tooled the car away from the curb. He drove slowly to the corner, then turned east and continued toward the river. He seemed to be in no hurry to get anywhere.

The woman sat twisted around in such a way that she faced Steve, with the pistol in her right hand still pointing at him. For many minutes she sat without speaking, just looking at him, studying him. The street lamps they passed cast swift and flickering lights across her face. It was impossible to guess the meaning of the expression in her tawny eyes.

Steve kept his left hand on the gun in his pocket. With his right he extracted a package of cigarettes, offered her one. She shook her head impatiently, as if annoyed that he should interrupt her study of him. Steve raised his eyebrows. He lit the cigarette, manipulating the book of matches with one hand. He said nothing, leaving the burden of opening the conversation to her.

It was only after he had got the cigarette going, and was exhaling a cloud of smoke, that she spoke.

"Captain Trent," she said, "in your pocket you have a certain miniature model of a 150-millimeter shell. I want it. Where we are going, the shell will be taken from you, and you will be killed. It would be better for you if you gave me the shell now. I would stop the car and you could step out and go away, a free man—and a live one."

Stephen Klaw smiled. "You're sure you wouldn't shoot me in the back as I left?"

"No," she said. "I give you my word I wouldn't shoot you in the back."

STEVE MET her glance, saw the eagerness in her eyes. It reminded him of the look he had seen in *Herr* Mueller's eyes a little while ago, when the big man's arm stretched out his hand and demanded the shell.

"Well?" she pressed. "What is your answer?"

Steve didn't reply at once. He took a long pull at the cigarette, let the smoke gather in his lungs, then sent a series of smoke rings into the air.

"Who sent you?" he asked her suddenly. "Venic? Or von Spegler himself?"

Her eyes flickered. "It doesn't matter who sent me. I want the shell. I'm giving you a chance for your life."

"No!" said Stephen Klaw. "I want fifty thousand dollars. That's what I was promised."

"You shall have it," she told him quickly. She picked up a small black bag which lay on the seat at her side. "The money is here. As soon as I have made sure of a certain thing about the shell, you may have your money."

"No!" Steve said once more. "I won't do business with anyone but von Spegler. Take me to him."

"I can't do that."

"Then you can't have the shell."

She gave him a commiserating smile. "You are surprisingly brave for a man who is betraying his country."

Steve said nothing.

She sighed. "I shall hate to see you die. Why must you be obstinate? The money is here for you."

"Open the bag," said Steve. "Let's see the color of that money."

She pushed the bag over to him. "Open it yourself. It isn't locked."

With his left hand Steve manipulated the catch. The bag fell open. It contained many packages, with money bands around them. On the outside of each package was a hundred-dollar bill. Steve picked up one of the packages and ripped the band off, still working only with his left hand. He flipped off the top bill and exposed blank paper underneath.

He looked up at her, grinning. "Well?" he asked.

Her cameo face was set and hard. "You are a fool, Captain Trent. Did you think that von Spegler intended to pay you fifty thousand dollars for that shell?"

"No," said Steve. "I guess not. There are ten packages in here, and each package has a hundred-dollar bill on top and bottom. That makes twenty of them, or two thousand dollars. That's all I would have got." He smiled tightly. "You people don't like to pay out, do you, Miss—er—Miss—"

He waited, and she supplied the name: "Alvarez. I am the Señorita Benita Alvarez. I am sorry that you saw the blank paper. It would have been better for you if you had handed over the shell."

"Thank you for worrying about me, Miss Benita Alvarez," Stephen Klaw said. "I think you're a hell of a nice girl when you're not working, and I hate to do this!"

He flipped the opened package of bills directly at her face. The blank sheets of paper fluttered in front of her eyes, and she instinctively raised her right hand to ward them off.

Steve reached over and took her wrist in his fingers, and held it high up, with the pistol pointing in the air. He gave her wrist a little twist, and she gasped and let go of the weapon. It fell to the seat between them.

HER FACE was white with fury and frustration. She tried to struggle, to claw at his face with her fingernails. Steve got both her slender wrists in his one hand, and held her off at arm's length.

She was panting with rage. "Basil!" she choked. *"Basil!"*

The car jerked to a sudden and jarring stop as Basil applied the brakes. He twisted around in his seat, bringing a long, heavy revolver over the ledge to point at Klaw.

Klaw did not move from where he sat. He brought the automatic out of his left-hand pocket and shot Basil between the eyes.

The Señorita Benita Alvarez became rigid at the sight of the neat little hole in the chauffeur's forehead. Basil's wide-open, dead eyes stared at them for a long minute, and a small trickle of blood wound its way down on the bridge of his nose. Then his body leaned over to one side in a ludicrous way. The head slumped forward, and he toppled over on the seat.

Klaw had retained his grip on the señorita's wrists. Now he released her, and picked up her small, vicious little gun. He let down the window and flung the gun out into the street.

"And now, Señorita," he said, "I shall leave you. It was a pleasant ride."

She sat quite still, her face white. She looked at him as if she were seeing him for the first time.

"Who are you?" she asked hoarsely. "You're more than a mere

army captain turned traitor. You think like a lightning streak, and you move more quickly. Who are you?"

Steve smiled. "Lady, for your purposes, I am merely the man who has *this!*"

He took the bronze shell out of his pocket, and showed it to her, then quickly put it back. "You may tell your precious von Spegler that I am staying at the Forge River Hotel. If he wants this shell, let him come and get it—in person."

He opened the door of the limousine, and stepped out into the street.

"Wait!" exclaimed the Señorita Alvarez.

Klaw stopped, raising his eyebrows.

She leaned forward, and spoke earnestly. "Captain Trent— or whoever you are—do not be a fool. You are a brave man, but your courage will do you no good. Those for whom I work are clever and ruthless, and they will stop at nothing. Give up that shell now. Do not thrust out your neck for the ax. Do not be foolhardy, or you will be dead before midnight!"

"Thank you," said Stephen Klaw. "And don't forget to give von Spegler my message."

He turned and walked away. And behind him he heard the Señorita Benita Alvarez's exasperated exclamation: "The fool! *Oh, the brave fool!*"

CHAPTER 4
FIFTEEN MINUTES TO LIVE

AS STEPHEN KLAW entered the lobby of the Forge Valley Hotel, he noted a certain tenseness in the air. There was a blocky, square-headed man standing near the desk; another, chewing a toothpick, over near the elevators. Several other people were in the lobby, but it was these two whom Steve noted especially, for the reason that they were both very careful not to look in his direction.

In making his way to the desk, he had to pass an armchair in which sat a little old man. His coat collar was turned up, and a muffler was wrapped around his throat as if he were afraid of catching cold. This old gentleman was wearing a weatherbeaten black slouch hat, whose brim was turned down over his face. Almost all that was visible between muffler and hatbrim was a long, sharp nose upon which rested a pair of steel-rimmed eyeglasses. He seemed to be immersed in a newspaper, and the hands which held it were sheathed in black gloves.

As Steve passed the armchair, the elderly gentleman said, *"Ahem!"*

Steve stopped. The old gentleman was looking up at him over the rims of the glasses.

"Young man," he asked, "can you tell me what time it is?"

Steve knew perfectly well that there was an electric clock directly over the desk in full view of the old gentleman if he turned his head. But something in the other's gaze impelled him to answer.

"A quarter after nine," he said. He waited, knowing there would be more. And there was.

"A quarter after nine, eh? Well, then, young man, you have fifteen minutes more of life!"

"How so?" Steve asked.

The old man chuckled. "That thing you're carrying around in your pocket—it's dynamite."

"What the hell are you talking about?" Steve demanded.

Once more that chuckle came from under the muffler. "Sit down, young man." He gestured toward the chair next to his. "Sit down and I'll tell you about it. Don't worry about those buzzards waiting for you at the desk and the elevator. They won't go away."

Stephen Klaw shrugged. He kept his narrowed eyes on the old man, and sat down in the adjacent chair.

"All right," he said. "I'm listening."

The old man turned toward him. He showed no more of his face than he had previously, but his eyes behind those thick lenses were steely bright. "The name is Trent," he said. "Does that mean anything to you?"

"Perhaps," Stephen Klaw said carefully.

The old man chuckled again. "You're going around calling yourself Paul Trent, aren't you? Well, you may fool all those others. You may fool Mueller, and Venic, and that dark-haired Alvarez woman—and even von Spegler himself. But you can't fool me. You see—" he leaned a little closer, allowing the muffler to fall away from his chin—"you see, *I am Paul Trent!*"

KLAW STIFFENED, watching the other, every fibre alert. That falling muffler had revealed the other's mouth and chin.

They were the features of a younger man. The tinting on the upper cheeks was artificial, making him appear sallow and old. In reality he was not old and feeble at all. And those glasses—they were certainly unnecessary, for the eyes behind them were keen and strong.

"That's right," he said, smiling wryly at Klaw. "I fooled you. I fooled them all—Mueller, and Venic, and von Spegler. If they knew who I am, I'd not live to leave this lobby. And you—you're taking it on the chin for me—posing as me!"

Stephen Klaw was thinking fast. Of course, he had vaguely imagined that there must be a real Captain Paul Trent somewhere or other. Why this Paul Trent was not appearing in person, he hadn't bothered to wonder. But now he did. As far as admitting that he wasn't Trent, he didn't mind that. Benita Alvarez already suspected that he wasn't Trent. She must have communicated her suspicions to her superiors by this time. It didn't matter who they thought he was—as long as they knew he still had the shell. They'd come to him for the shell, no matter what name he used. But he wanted to know more about this man who sat next to him. He studied the fellow's face. Was he really a traitor? Had he really been ready to sell out the United States? And had his sister circumvented him somehow?

Trent's face did not seem to be that of a weakling or a traitor. Rather, it was strong and intelligent, somehow giving the impression of a studious dreamer, a visionary. There was a little scar along the left side of his chin, barely visible.

Trent saw him looking at it, and smiled. "I got that experimenting with picric acid." He leaned forward. "Look here—

whatever your name is. I'm going to tell you something. I'm a damned coward. *I* was supposed to come to the Continental Café with that shell, but I didn't have the guts to go through with it. So Nancy, my sister, had to get someone else. She got you. But you spoiled everything by refusing to give them the shell. I was there. I saw everything."

Stephen Klaw frowned. "What do you mean? Was I supposed to give it to them?"

Trent groaned. "Didn't Nancy tell you?"

"No. She didn't have time."

"Good Lord!"

Steve watched him closely. "What did you mean before, when you said I had only fifteen minutes to live?"

"That's it! That's what I meant!" He looked up quickly at the clock. It showed twenty-two after nine. "I've got to tell you quickly, or it'll be too late. I worked out the trick to get von Spegler and his whole damned spying organization and blow them to hell.

"That shell model is supposed to have all the interior mechanism worked out to scale, so their engineers back in Germany can make blueprints from it and start production at once. But I took out all that mechanism, and put in something a whole lot different. I put in a delicate watch mechanism, and hooked it up with a supercharged miniature battery. The battery and the watch mechanism take up just half the interior of that shell. Do you know what's in the rest of it? Lyddite!

"I put a half pound of lyddite in there—enough to blow up this whole damned lobby, and kill everyone in it. I figured that it would be placed in the hands of von Spegler at just about nine-thirty. That's when it's timed to go up. *And you've got just seven minutes to get rid of it!*"

"I see," said Steve. "And how do you suggest that I get rid of it?"

"Throw it away. Throw it out in the street: Or—here, let me have it. I can stop the timing device!"

Stephen Klaw made no move to take the shell out of his pocket. "I'm sorry," he lied. "I should have told you before I haven't got the shell any more."

"You—you haven't got it!" Trent's eyes bored at Steve through the steel-rimmed spectacles. "What did you do with it?"

"That woman got it—Señorita Benita Alvarez. She picked me up in a car, and took it away from me at the point of a gun."

"Oh, Lord!" Trent groaned. "That's terrible!"

"Why is it terrible?" Steve asked. "Isn't it just what you wanted? She'll give it to von Spegler, no doubt." Klaw's eyes were blank.

"No, no, you don't understand. She doesn't work for von Spegler. She's—"

ABRUPTLY HE leaped up from his armchair, wrapping the muffler around his face. "I must go! Maybe it isn't too late!" He turned his collar up, threw the newspaper down on the chair, and almost ran out to the street, without once looking back.

Steve didn't attempt to stop him. He watched him go, frowning. Then he turned and saw that the man at the desk and the one at the elevators were watching him furtively. He gave no sign that he had noticed them, and glanced up at the electric clock. It showed twenty-six minutes after nine.

He walked across the lobby to the lavatory, and went inside without looking back. As soon as he was inside, he stepped into the corner alongside the door, so that if the door were opened, he would be behind it. Then he took out the shell, and examined it. There were three places where parts had been joined together. He tried unscrewing the end one with the flat base, and it came off.

There was no clockwork mechanism on the inside. Neither was there a miniature battery, or any lyddite. But there was a roll of thin parchment. It crackled as he unrolled it.

He stared at it, with a puzzled frown. There was nothing on the parchment, except for an emblem at the top—an eagle surmounted by a swastika. Otherwise, the sheet of parchment was blank.

Just then the door was pushed open violently. It opened all the way, screening him from the view of the two men who barged in. They were the two who had been watching in the lobby. As they entered, they brought guns out from under their coats, and rushed into the lavatory. The kicked open the doors of the small booths, holding their guns ready. And when they found no one in there, they turned and looked bewilderedly at each other.

Stephen Klaw swiftly put away the unscrewed parts of the shell, and the blank parchment. He thrust his hands into his pockets. Then he smiled grimly.

"Were you looking for me, gentlemen?" he asked.

The two men jumped as if they had stepped on fire. They

swung around, jerking up their guns. They saw Steve, and one of them said, "Ach!" and pulled the trigger of his gun. The other one fired at the same instant. But they were both a split-second slower than Stephen Klaw, who had brought both his automatics out of his pockets. He shot with both guns at the same time, so that they made only a single sound.

The two men slammed back against the tiled wall, one with a bullet in his throat, the other with a slug through his heart. Their own shots ricocheted off the tiles on either side of Klaw. They had had their guns out and in their hands, while Steve was just pulling his from his pockets. Yet they hadn't been able to shoot quickly enough.

Steve pocketed his automatics. He did not look at the two men. He screwed the bottom end on the shell, and slipped the rolled strip of blank parchment into his vest pocket. Then he opened the door of the men's room and stepped out into the lobby.

One or two people were looking around, wondering where the explosions had come from. They had seemed rather loud for the backfiring of a car. Seeing Steve come out of the lavatory so calmly, they had no suspicion that the sounds had come from there.

He strolled over to the desk and asked for his key.

THE CLERK acted ill at ease. He fumbled the key twice before he got it out of the pigeon hole and onto the desk. "H—here you are, C-captain Trent. Room 901." He tore a slip of paper from his memo pad, and gave it to Steve.

"And there is a t-telephone message that j-just came in while you were in the lavatory, Captain. A young lady phoned. She wouldn't give her name, and she said she couldn't wait to talk with you. She said t-to be sure and give you the message at once, before you went upstairs."

Klaw raised his eyebrows, and took the paper. It was an ordinary telephone memo slip, with the time and message written in pencil by the clerk:

Time of Call: *9:28 P.M.*
For: *Captain Paul Trent*
Room Number: *901*
Message: *Do not go up to your room. Danger. Meet me at Forge River Ammunition Plant, 10 o'clock sharp, northeast entrance. Come on foot, and armed. Be careful. If I am not there by five after ten, go right in and find Shell Storage Chamber Number One. Don't fail me. And above all, don't go up to your room!*
Name of Party Leaving Message: *N. T.*

Steve read the message over twice. *N. T.*— Nancy Trent! The girl who had posed as his sister in the Continental Café. The girl who had given him the shell.

He looked up, to find the clerk watching him.

"She wouldn't give her name, sir. She said you'd recognize the initials."

"Did she have a low, husky voice?" Steve asked. "Or a clear, musical one?"

"It—it wasn't husky, sir. Very clear, and businesslike. Now that you mention it, there was a sort of musical lilt to it. Very pleasant, sir, in spite of the nature of the message."

The clerk leaned over the counter and lowered his voice. "You know, Captain, I'm worried—about that part warning you not to go up to your room. S-shall I ask the house detective to look into it?"

"Not at all," said Steve. "It's probably a practical joke. Don't worry about it at all. There won't be any trouble."

"I'm very glad to hear that, sir. I—I was afraid there was some monkey business going on—those two men who were watching you. One of them stood here, and the other by the elevator. Then, when you got through talking to that elderly gentleman, they followed you into the lavatory. They—they didn't annoy you?"

"Oh, no!" Steve told him. "They were no trouble at all. I can assure you that they're both very peaceful gentlemen right now."

"I'm so glad to hear that, sir!" the clerk said, with a look of relief.

Steve gave him a smile, and started for the elevators. Then he remembered something, and stopped.

"What room have Mr. Kerrigan and Mr. Murdoch?"

"Room 903, sir. They reserved the room next to yours."

"Thanks. If they come in, send them right up. If they phone, connect them with me immediately."

He crossed over to the elevator, and got in.

At the ninth floor, he threw a swift glance to the right and the left along the corridor as he stepped out of the cage.

It was fortunate that he did so.

CHAPTER 5
WITH THE COMPLIMENTS
OF JAPAN

O RDINARILY, A man would not have looked to the left, when his room was down the corridor to the right. The average man, on leaving the elevator, will turn in the direction in which he must go. Had Stephen Klaw done so, he would not have seen the ungainly silencer on the end of the rifle barrel which was sticking out of the crack of the partly opened door of Room 930.

As it was, he glimpsed it almost before the door of the cage had slid shut behind him with its oily, staccato click.

Klaw had lived dangerously enough to have developed a set of instinctive reactions to certain stimuli. Psychologists, giving them the name of *conditioned reflexes,* assert that persons can be trained to perform definite reflex actions in response to definite stimuli. They have performed hundreds of experiments to prove this theory. For instance, they have allowed a child to burn its hand on a hot poker. For ever after, that child will jerk his hand backward when he is shown a poker. They call this a reflex, which was not inherited by the child, but which had been developed by conditions.

Stephen Klaw didn't bother his head about conditioned reflex, or about psychological verbiage like "hereditary" or "environmental." He knew, without having to think about it, that a silenced rifle barrel poking out at him from behind a partly opened door meant only one thing. And he didn't have to dig up five-syllable words, to find a name for that thing. He acted.

All he heard was a little *plop* from the silenced rifle. All he saw was a quick flash of flame from the hole in the silencer. He got only that fleeting glimpse of it, because he was already in a headlong dive for the floor.

There was a nice, thick carpet underfoot, and he landed without too much of a jar, on his hands. There was a splintering and crashing of glass as the bullet from the silenced rifle struck the glass of the elevator door. The glass splashed out into the shaft, tinkling against the steel struts.

Steve rolled over once, as another shot *zinged* past him. The sniper behind the door of 930 had tried another quick one when he saw his first shot miss. But he didn't fly another, because Stephen Klaw had come to his feet in a bounce, with two automatics in his hands. Steve's fingers were on the triggers, but he didn't shoot. The silenced rifle muzzle had disappeared from the crack, and the door of 930 started to close.

Klaw hurled himself forward along the hall in a lightning sprint, and reached the door just as it banged shut. He twisted the knob, and hurled himself against it.

Whoever was on the other side hadn't had time to snap the lock, for the door gave under Steve's impact, and he went catapulting through.

The door swung wide open, and struck the man inside. As Steve came through he got a glimpse of a little fellow, no more than five-feet-two, staggering backward and clawing for balance, the silenced rifle spinning out of his hands.

Steve's eyes narrowed. The fellow was a Japanese.

He was a small, lithe man, well-muscled and agile. But he wasn't agile enough to maintain his balance. He sprawled on the floor, grunting.

Steve kicked the door shut, and put his guns away.

"All right," he said. "You can get up."

THE JAPANESE got to his feet, looking somewhat shame-faced. He had a high forehead, and small, shrewdly clever eyes.

"So sorry, Captain Trent," he said. "The mistake was entirely mine."

Steve grinned. "You mean the mistake you made when you missed me with the rifle?"

"Exactly!" The Japanese smiled, revealing two beautiful rows of false teeth.

He straightened his coat, turning down the collar, which had become rumpled. He bowed low, while he continued to fix his collar.

"My aim was disgraceful," he said apologetically. "But I assure you that it shall be better this time!"

He came erect with a small pistol in his hand, which he had produced from somewhere under his coat. He was no longer smiling.

Stephen Klaw saw the glitter of metal even as the fellow was coming erect. He was already in motion. He reached the Japanese in a single leap, and brought the edge of his right hand down upon the wrist of the Japanese.

There was no sound to the blow, but a spasm of pain raced across the yellow face, and the man let the pistol drop.

"Your second mistake!" Steve said, grinning, and kicked the pistol under the bureau.

The Japanese veiled his eyes. "Captain Trent," he said, "I see that you are a far more dangerous man than I had been led to believe."

"Thank you," said Steve. "Now, maybe you'll tell me why you're so anxious to put a slug in me."

The Jap shrugged. "You should know that better than I, Captain Trent. Search your conscience. Have you no reason to fear the wrath of the Imperial Japanese Government?"

Steve looked at him blankly. "Who are you?" he demanded.

The other bowed jerkily. "Forgive me. I have forgotten the first rules of politeness. One must be polite—must one not?—even with a man one intends to kill. I am Lieutenant Suzuke Inyo, lieutenant in the Imperial Military Intelligence Service of our glorious Emperor."

"Ah!" said Steve. "And your purpose is to kill me?"

"That is my duty. It was an order. I am to kill you, and take from you that thing which you wish to sell to—certain others. If I fail, Captain Trent, my own life is forfeit. This much explanation I feel I owe you for that which I am about to do!"

As he spoke his knees bent slightly, and then he straightened them in a leap that sent his whole body catapulting at Steve. The first and second fingers of his right hand were thrust out, aiming for Steve's eyes.

It was an old oriental trick, and it had brought about the death of many an unprepared man in its time. The trick was not to blind the victim with those two outstretched fingers, but to concentrate all of his attention upon them, while the left hand drew a knife and slashed upward in a deadly disemboweling stroke.

This is what Suzuke Inyo now did.

Stephen Klaw had never seen that trick before. But he had heard of it. He did not react in the orthodox, expected fashion. Any man whose eyes are threatened by those two vicious, outthrust fingers will instinctively throw up an arm to ward them off, thus leaving his torso open to the knife attack.

Stephen Klaw didn't do that. Instead, he dropped his head and came in to meet the attack, with both fists driving one-two punches at the Jap's solar plexus. Two things happened simultaneously. Inyo's outthrust fingers broke with a terrible, crunching sound, against the top of Klaw's skull. And Klaw's right sleeve caught the blade of the knife. It ripped through the sleeve, and gashed his forearm.

Suzuke Inyo fell away, with an involuntary gasp of pain because of his two terribly broken fingers. He let go of the knife, and it fell to the floor. For a minute he stood, bent over, taut with agony pressing his hand against his chest and breathing heavily. HE RAISED his eyes to Steve's, and there was no hatred in them. Only admiration. He spoke through lips that were compressed with pain.

"Captain Trent, sir, accept the humble compliments of Suzuke Inyo. You, sir, are a superior man. It has been my privilege to be a member of the Military Intelligence of my country for fifteen years. I am accounted the most efficient operative of the service. No man has ever been able to say that he got the best of Suzuke

Inyo—until tonight. In you, sir, I have met my match. More than that—my master!"

"That's a very nice speech, Lieutenant," Steve said, dabbing a handkerchief at his cut arm, "and I thank you for it. I'd like to help you with those broken fingers, but I'm wondering if you're ready to call it quits, or will you try again while I'm helping you?"

Suzuke Inyo smiled painfully. "If you were in my place—with orders to kill a man or not return—would you stop?"

"No," said Steve.

"There you have your answer, Captain Trent."

Inyo's face was twitching with his pain. His hand was swelling above his broken fingers.

Steve said impatiently, "Look here, Inyo. Would it be against your orders to call a ten-minute truce? An armistice? I could fix up your fingers in ten minutes."

Inyo was swaying just a little. "Perhaps—perhaps I could do that. But only with the understanding that I will try to kill you again as soon as the ten minutes are over."

"Agreed!" said Stephen Klaw.

He kicked the knife out of the way, and helped Inyo to a chair. "H'm," he said. "Those fingers are broken in half a dozen places. You'll need a doctor. All I can do is fix them up for the time being. They must hurt like hell."

"Indeed they do, Captain Trent. Is it not strange that broken fingers should—affect me so, when I have stood up under the shock of being hit by .45 calibre bullets? I suppose it is because the fingers, being intended to transmit impressions by the sense of touch, are so sensitive—"

He broke off, biting his lip, as Steve yanked at the bones, trying to set them back roughly in place. The little Jap sat stoically while Steve worked over him.

At last Steve said, "Well, that'll have to do till you can see a doctor, Inyo. Hold that hand up in the air for a minute."

He tore strips from the bedsheet and, using a pencil as a splint, began to tie the fingers tightly in a bandage.

Inyo had mastered the pain somewhat. He sat, looking up at Steve, quizzically.

"You are a strange man, Captain Trent. A strange, brave and foolish man, to help your enemy. Why do you do this for me, knowing that I intend to kill you?"

Steve shrugged. "Maybe it's because I liked the way you talked, warning me, before you jumped me just now."

"There is something else I am wondering about," said the little Jap. "I was told that you were a coward, and a traitor to your country. I was told that, having sold a certain thing to a Japanese agent, you stole it back from him, and then made a deal to sell it to the Germans and the Russians as well."

"Really!" said Steve, winding the bandage tight. "You were certainly told a lot about me!"

"And that is the strange thing about which I am wondering," Suzuke Inyo persisted doggedly. "No man who fights as you fight, or who acts as you are now acting, can be a coward and a traitor. Therefore, sir, I draw the conclusion *that you are not Captain Trent!*"

STEVE DIDN'T answer. He finished tying the knot in the bandage, and stepped back. He looked at his wrist watch.

"The ten minute truce is over, Lieutenant Suzuke Inyo," he said. "Are you ready to try again?"

The Jap remained in his chair. He smiled, and shook his head.

"In our business," he said, "one must learn to judge men, to make quick and accurate decisions, and to act accordingly. I have decided that you are not Captain Trent. Therefore, you are not the man I am ordered to kill. Whoever you are, you are neither a traitor nor a coward. You must be an agent of the American Government, posing as Trent. Please tell me if I am right, for it is important to both of us."

He leaned forward, holding his bandaged hand up in the air. "Believe me, sir, I speak only the truth now. If you have in your possession the thing which the others are seeking, *it is to the interest of my Service to see that you keep it!*"

His thin, yellow face was utterly earnest and sincere.

Steve studied him for a long minute. Then he nodded. "All right, Inyo, I'm going to trust you—partially. I am not Captain Trent. I am Stephen Klaw, of the Federal Bureau of Investigation."

Suzuke Inyo's bland eyes began to glitter. A little hissing sigh escaped him.

"I am glad to hear that, Stephen Klaw. It is a relief to know that I was bested by such a one as you. Never fear, I have heard of you and of your two partners, Kerrigan and Murdoch. The Suicide Squad—is not that what you are called, you three?"

Steve inclined his head. "We've been called that." He waved his hand to dismiss the subject. "Now maybe you'll tell me where you fit into the picture?"

Suzuke Inyo's eyes were bland. "There is one thing I must ask you. The shell—you have it?"

"I have it."

"With you?"

"Yes."

"May I see it?"

"No, Lieutenant."

The Jap shrugged. "It is too bad that we cannot trust each other more fully. I could be of great help to you. I know of a great danger that threatens your country tonight. But if you will not trust me, we must work separately. I can only tell you that it is my purpose to prevent that shell, and its contents, from being turned over to those others who want it. Keep it very safely, Stephen Klaw."

"You can stop worrying, Lieutenant," Steve told him. "The shell will not get into the hands of von Spegler."

"Or of Madame Vorovna, either!" the Jap exclaimed eagerly. "Do not underestimate the Russians, Stephen Klaw. They are as dangerous as von Spegler. Madame Vorovna is their chief agent here. She, too, wants that secret."

"Madame Vorovna?" Steve asked. "What's she like?"

"As beautiful as a siren," Inyo told him. "And as dangerous as a cobra. She is dark, and sensuous, mistress of passions as well as men. She speaks a dozen languages, and has passed for a Spaniard, an Italian, a Bulgarian and a French woman."

"Ah," said Steve. "I think I've had the pleasure of meeting her."

He opened the door. "Goodbye, Lieutenant," he said. "Have no further fears for that shell."

AS STEVE stepped out into the hall, he saw Suzuke Inyo watching him with a curious, wondering expression.

He walked down the hall with both hands in his pockets, but he did not turn around once. He hadn't taken the silenced rifle from Inyo's room. If he had misjudged the Jap, he would never hear the report. The first thing he'd know about it would be when the slug smashed into his back between the shoulder blades. But he kept himself rigidly from turning around.

He passed the door of 903, which was the room assigned to Dan Murdoch and Johnny Kerrigan. He wondered if they had returned yet, but he refrained from rapping at their door. He remembered the note from Nancy Trent. She had warned him not to go to his room. She had hinted at danger. Had she meant the Jap? He doubted it. He thought that she must have referred to some other danger *in his room.* His mind began to click.

He approached the door of 901. He kept his left hand in his pocket, and with his right hand he took out the hotel key, which he inserted in the lock. He turned it, and pushed open the door.

His room was in darkness, as he had left it. But even before he crossed the threshold he sensed some alien presence there. His left hand tightened on the butt of the automatic in his pocket. With his right hand he pressed the button-catch in the door, so that it would not lock when he closed it. Then he stepped inside.

Almost at once, there was a rush of bodies in the darkness.

Someone slammed the door shut. Someone else reached for his throat, while others tried to seize his arms. He twisted to one side, and heard a blackjack swish past his ear. It struck his shoulder, but he was moving with the blow, and it didn't bother him much. He brought up one knee, hard, and elicited a grunt of agony as it sank home.

He smashed a fist into a face, and brought out his left hand, with the automatic. He didn't shoot, but used it as a club, and felt the gun-sight rake across bone.

But they were bearing him down by sheer weight of numbers.

Someone uttered a guttural command in German, and they renewed the attack ever more fiercely. Blows rained down on Steve from all sides. He parried them in the dark, fighting coldly, automatically, giving value for everything he received. But he was only one, and they were many.

A knife blade slithered past his neck, and a pair of brass knuckles grazed his cheek.

The darkness favored him, for his attackers were in constant danger of striking one another. They must have realized this, for suddenly the lights came on.

Steve saw two men lying quite still on the floor, and another writhing in agony, with hands pressed against his groin. But there were five or six more pressing close about Steve. And the little man with the withered arm, Venic, was standing near the electric light switch. It was he who had turned on the lights.

He was holding a Krupp-Scheidemann light machine-gun under his good arm, with his finger curled around the trip, and the snout of the weapon pointed directly at Stephen Klaw. At a command from him, the attacking men leaped away, leaving a cleared space in front of Steve.

STEVE SWUNG his automatic to bear on Venic. If he was going to take a burst of lead from that Krupp-Scheidemann in his chest, he would at least put one slug into Venic. He was on the point of pressing the trigger when Venic shouted, "Wait!"

The other men stood motionless in the room while Venic and Stephen Klaw faced each other, at the points of their weapons. Venic's eyes were hot and glittering, Klaw's slate-gray and cold.

"Good evening, Captain Trent," Venic said. "Shall we talk—before we shoot?"

Steve didn't move, except to watch the other men out of the corners of his eyes, at the same time they studied Venic for that first flicker of the eyelids which would telegraph a warning that he intended to press the trip of the machine gun.

"Go ahead and talk," he said. "I'm listening."

Venic's lips twisted in a crooked smile. "We could have killed you as you stepped into the room, Captain Trent. The light from the hall was behind you, making you an excellent target. A single burst from this little plaything of mine would have done the trick."

Steve grinned, keeping his automatic steady. "Don't tell me you held your fire because you liked the way I part my hair."

"Hardly that, Captain Trent. We merely wished to make sure you had the shell with you. It is that which we want, rather than your life. Possibly *Herr* Mueller may bear you a grudge for what you did to him in the Continental Café. But not I. I only want the shell. Have you still got it with you?"

"If I tell you I have—then you pull the trip of that machine-gun?"

"Not necessarily. You can hand over the shell, and you will be allowed to leave this room alive. Otherwise—" he shrugged—

"this Krupp-Scheidemann can fire twenty rounds a second. Twenty rounds will leave you very dead."

Steve's eyes flickered, "on the other hand," he said softly, "suppose we put it this way. You can order your so-called tough babies here, to walk out of my room in a nice, refined way. And you get the hell out of here with them. Otherwise—" Steve shrugged in imitation of Venic's gesture—"this little automatic of mine will fire one shot, which will hit you squarely between the eyes. And I assure you, my dear Mr. Venic, that it will leave you just as dead as I!"

"In that case, Captain Trent," whispered Venic, "we shall both be dead!" And his finger tightened on the trip.

CHAPTER 6
BARGAIN WITH DEATH

S O TENSE was everyone in the room that nobody saw the door inching open behind Stephen Klaw. Venic's hand was actually against the trip of the machine-gun, and Steve was already shooting, when a little *plop* sounded, through the open crack in the doorway.

The *plop* was immediately drowned out by the thunder of Steve's automatic. But it was that single shot from the silenced rifle in the hands of Lieutenant Suzuke Inyo which saved Klaw's life. Inyo had fired a split-second before either of them.

The shot caught Venic in the throat and he threw up his hands as it hurled him backward. The machine-gun began to spit slugs into the ceiling. For only an instant did Venic's body arc backward, then it was straightened by the powerful drive of Steve's bullet, above the heart. Steve had intended to shoot for Venic's elbow, on the off-chance of deflecting the machine-gun burst. But Inyo's shot had swung him out of line, and he took the bullet in his heart.

Steve didn't wait to see who had fired through the doorway, but he guessed from the muffled explosion, that it was the Jap's rifle. He threw himself at Venic's falling body, and snatched the machine-gun. At the same time, Inyo kicked the door open and began to pump more shots from the silenced rifle into the group of men in the center of the room.

They were already shooting, but Inyo dropped two of them, and when Steve turned the Krupp-Scheidemann on them they threw away their weapons in a fervor of fear, and raised their hands high above their heads.

Suzuke Inyo came into the room, smiling and showing all his white teeth. He put his injured hand to his side, and swayed. But he kept on smiling. He brought the hand away, and it was wet with blood seeping from a wound just under the heart.

"I am so glad, Stephen Klaw," he said in a whisper, "that I— was able—to help you—"

His knees buckled, and he keeled over.

At the same instant there was the sound of running feet in the corridor and Dan Murdoch burst into the room. He had a gun in his hand, but he lowered it when he saw that everything was under control.

"Shrimp!" he barked. "You all right?"

"Yes," Steve snapped. "Watch the birds!"

He let Murdoch cover the prisoners, and bent down at the side of Lieutenant Suzuke Inyo.

The Japanese lieutenant was breathing with difficulty. He gave Steve a wan smile. "You still have—the shell—safe?"

"Yes."

"That—is good. I have—only a moment—to live. Ask them to send—my body back to—Nippon. Tell them—I died in the course of—duty."

"I'll tell them, Inyo," Steve whispered. "I'll surely tell them."

"Then I—have nothing to—wait for. Only this—you must keep that—secret from von Spegler and Madame—Vorovna. My country wishes to keep your country—out of the war. If I have helped accomplish that—I shall not have died in vain."

"Don't worry, Inyo. You've done your duty."

"No, no. Listen closely. There—was a plot. The Germans wanted the secret of the shells. They made—an alliance with the Russians. When they get the secret—they will destroy the—Forge River Ammunition Plant—so that your country cannot furnish the same shells to—England and France. The plot is for tonight. Even if they fail to get the secret, they will blow up the ammunition plant!"

Steve bent closer. "You're sure?"

"Yes, yes. You must stop them…."

His breath left his body in a great gasp, and he died.

GENTLY, STEVE laid his head down, and then got to his feet. "Dan," he said, "there was a man you'd have been proud to know!"

Murdoch had been busy tying the prisoners, using strips of

the bedsheet. "Good Lord," he murmured, looking down at the dead man. "A Jap! We're running into every damn thing on this job. Russians, Germans—and now a Jap. And we're no nearer to von Spegler!"

"Where's Johnny?" Steve demanded.

"He's following up another angle," Dan told him. "We turned *Herr* Mueller in to the police, and they booked him on a charge of disorderly conduct. Then Johnny and I worked our way out to the rear, after you. You were gone, and we began combing the place for the other chap you mentioned—Venic."

Steve nodded toward the body of the man with the withered arm. "There he is."

Murdoch grunted. "We didn't know. We couldn't find him, so we tried that alley out in back, and when we reached the back street, we saw an old guy in a turned-up collar and muffler and eyeglasses. He had a cab, and he was snooping around, with the cab waiting for him. Pretty soon, a limousine drove up. The funny part of it was that a dame was driving that limousine. She was a knockout. She waved to old Snoopy-brows, and they jabbered a while, and we heard the old guy say Donnervetter, it was a shame, and that his men would take care of the American, and he and the dame had better go and finish the girl and the other business. He paid off the cab and got in the limousine and she drove away."

"I met them both!" Stephen Klaw exclaimed. "The old guy is a young fellow made up that way. And the woman is a Russian who's posing as a Spaniard. What did you do?"

"I told Johnny to grab that cab and tail them, and I came here pronto, to see if by any chance you were the American they were talking about."

"I was," Steve said grimly. He looked at his wrist watch. "It's five of ten, and I've got a date at the Forge River Ammo Plant at ten o'clock. Let's be going, Dan. I think it'll be a hot night tonight."

"Suits me," Dan Murdoch said sourly. "You've been getting all the gravy so far."

They left the prisoners tied on the floor, with the two dead bodies, and hurried out into the corridor. There were several people out there, all watching the door of 901, and chattering with excitement. One of them shouted that they had phoned down to the desk for the riot squad. The elevator indicator was rising, showing that the call was being answered.

Steve dragged Dan Murdoch toward the fire-exit. "We'll have to leg it down," he whispered. "We haven't any time for explanations!"

No one offered to stop them, but Dan took enough time to show one of the crowd his F.B.I. badge, and to explain swiftly that this was government business. Then they made for the exit.

They went down two flights, and caught a down elevator, while the cage which had been on the way up was unloading at the ninth. They reached the lobby and started for the front door. **STEPHEN KLAW** suddenly yanked Murdoch back behind a pillar. "Is that the dame you saw in the limousine?" he demanded, pointing at the revolving doors.

"That's the one!" said Dan.

The woman who called herself Benita Alvarez was just entering the lobby. Since the time when Stephen Klaw had shot her chauffeur and walked away from her, she had found an opportunity to apply fresh make-up, and to fix her hair. She looked as self-possessed and cool as if she were scheduled for an evening at the theatre instead of being engaged in the most dangerous and ruthless business in the world.

She made straight for the elevators. Stephen Klaw whispered to Dan to keep in the background, and stepped out from behind the pillar.

When she saw him, she stopped short, and smiled. That slow, languorous smile of hers was meant to inflame the minds and the hearts of men. But it left Steve cold. He was thinking of what Suzuke Inyo had told him about this woman.

"Good evening, Madame Vorovna!" he said.

"How do you do, my mysterious friend," she responded, throatily. "I was coming to see you. How fortunate that I did not miss you. Have you been up—to your room yet?"

"Why, yes."

"You—er—had no trouble there?"

"Trouble? Hardly any, Madame Vorovna. Just a few of your friends, who became a bit too boisterous."

She was watching him keenly. "Did they—did you—" She hesitated for a second, and Steve finished for her.

"Did they get the shell? No. They did not."

"Then perhaps we can do business. I know now that you are not Captain Trent. But you have the shell, and that is all that matters."

Steve glanced at the electric clock over the desk. It showed ten P.M. He frowned. He should have been at the Forge River plant by this time. But this woman might be the necessary link to von Spegler.

"I will do business with you," the woman hurried on. "I will trade you—the shell for the life of the Trent girl!"

Steve grew taut. But his face showed nothing. "What do you mean?"

She smiled. "The Trent girl is a—shall we say, hostage? Though we know now that you are not her brother, we also know that you were interested enough in her to risk your life for her by going into the Continental Café and posing as Paul Trent when you knew that the Japanese government had ordered Paul Trent's death. Also, when you knew that it meant death to defy von Spegler."

"Granted," said Steve. "I'm interested in her. What then?"

"She is a prisoner. Von Spegler is no respecter of sex. He can kill a woman as well as a man. If Venic and those others failed to get the shell from you, then I am authorized to offer you the girl's life in exchange for it. She dies in thirty minutes, unless I return with the shell."

Steve smiled grimly. "Madame Vorovna," he said, "permit me to introduce myself. I am Stephen Klaw, Special Agent of the Department of Justice. You have told me enough, in your own words, to convict you of espionage, of conspiracy against the United States Government, of attempted murder, and of kidnaping. Therefore, by virtue of the authority vested in me by the Department of Justice of the United States of America, I arrest you!"

SHE WAS not frightened, in spite of the fact that he had made it as impressive as he could. She laughed softly. "Stephen Klaw! I've heard of you, of course. I should have guessed, when those two fire-eaters appeared to rescue you at the Continental Café. Von Spegler has been wracking his brains, ever since he decided you weren't Captain Trent, to find who you really were."

"Come along," Steve said.

He took her arm, as if he were escorting her to the theatre, and led her toward the door. Behind them, Dan Murdoch saunted along, with an appearance of nonchalance, but actually scanning every person in the lobby with an eagle eye. He had overheard the conversation from his vantage point behind the pillar. And he knew that a woman like this one would not have come to make a deal with Klaw unless she were well protected. She must have foreseen that she would be laying herself open to arrest, and must have brought along a bodyguard of thugs for just such an emergency.

But no one attempted to stop them in the lobby. Steve squeezed into the same compartment of the revolving door with her, and Dan kept close behind.

At the curb, stood the limousine she had used before. Another chauffeur now sat behind the wheel, in place of Basil. And behind it was a second car, occupied by four men.

The woman raised her hand in signal to that car, and the four men piled out of it. They surged toward Stephen Klaw.

From behind him, Dan Murdoch said, "Keep going, Shrimp. This is my party!"

There was a happy gleam in his dark eyes. His hands moved

with the swiftness of a bird's flapping wings, and two guns appeared in them.

The four men saw this second menace, and swung their weapons toward Dan, while Steve calmly forced Benita Alvarez, alias Madame Vorovna, toward the limousine.

Dan Murdoch stood spraddle-legged in the middle of the sidewalk, with a set smile upon his handsome face, and squeezed the triggers of his two guns in deadly unison. Blast after blast spurted from those twin, flaming muzzles of his, smashing into the bodies of the four close-packed gunmen. The two in front fell at once, and the other two returned his fire, but without accuracy.

They weren't used to this sort of battle, and they had no stomach for it. They had anticipated only a quick scuffle with a single man, and here they found themselves facing an armed devil who had fire in his eyes and the smile of an avenging angel upon his lips. The third one fell with two bullets in his chest, hardly a half-inch apart, and the fourth one turned to run.

Dan Murdoch laughed out loud, and started to return his guns to their holsters. It was at that moment that the fleeing, thug chose to turn around and try a pot shot at him.

Dan was caught flat-footed. The barrels of both his guns were halfway back in the holsters. The thug's gun was already sighted at him. He'd never have time to draw his weapons and shoot before the other could pull the trigger.

Murdoch stood straight, with his head up, and faced the killer. It was his own fault, and he knew how to take it.

THE MAN, seeing Dan's helplessness, grinned nastily, and started to clamp down on the trigger. But he never fired, because Stephen Klaw, from the running-board of the limousine, nonchalantly triggered the gun in the left-hand pocket off his jacket. The slug smashed into the side of the man's face, carrying away most of it, and the fellow was hurled down to the pavement, a bloody, lifeless mass.

Dan Murdoch wiped sweat from his forehead. "Nice shooting, Shrimp," he said.

Stephen Klaw grinned. "I could have shot him about a second and a half sooner. But I wanted to teach you a lesson—never quit a fight till you've won."

Dan scowled at him. "If we weren't on duty, Shrimp, I'd wipe the floor with you!"

A crowd had gathered in front of the hotel. Madame Vorovna was sitting quite still inside the limousine, but the chauffeur had seized the opportunity to jump out from behind the wheel and try to make his escape. He started to zigzag across the street through the moving traffic and his panic brought him squarely in front of a car. The machine hit him with a terrible whacking sound, like the slap of a carpet beater against a rug. Brakes screeched. Traffic became snarled. A cop came running over from a police car parked across the street. It was this car which had answered the call about the shooting on the ninth floor, and he was waiting for his partner to come down.

While Dan Murdoch watched Madame Vorovna, Stephen Klaw took the cop aside and established his identity, told him a little of what was afoot. "I'm afraid they're going to destroy the Forge River Ammo Plant," he finished. "And if I have this thing figured right, there's a spunky little girl who's going to die at the same time. I've got to get over there fast. Cover this report, will you, and tell your precinct Captain that we'll be back to sign the records."

"My Gawd," said the cop, "lemme call the riot squad. We'll come down on the Forge River plant like a ton of bricks."

"That's just what we can't do," Steve interrupted. "From what this woman tells me, they've got the time set for ten-thirty. But if they see a raiding squad, what's to stop them from setting it off at once?"

The cop scratched his head. "I don't know if I ought to pass this up. It's too big for just two or three guys to handle—"

"You have nothing to do with it," Steve told him coldly. "This is a federal matter, and it's out of your jurisdiction. What you *can* do—give us twenty minutes' start, *then* send the raiding squad."

He started for the limousine, and the cop grabbed his sleeve.

"But—but how'll we know how you make out?"

Steve grinned sourly. "If you hear a hell of a big explosion in twenty minutes, you'll know we didn't make out so good!"

He nodded to Dan, who closed the door and remained inside with Madame Vorovna. Steve went around in front and got behind the wheel. He put the big car in gear and drove off, leaving the cop staring after them and scratching his head.

CHAPTER 7
FIVE MINUTES FROM INFERNO

THE FORGE River plant was only a six-minute drive from the center of town, across the Center Valley Bridge.

Madame Vorovna sat very stiff and very silent, her hands clenching and unclenching nervously. Ever since she had learned that she was up against the Suicide Squad, her self-assurance had dissipated. She made no resistance when Dan Murdoch, with profuse apologies, searched her thoroughly for hidden weapons. He found a wicked little sawed-off pistol stuck in a cute sheath in the top of her stocking. Her bag yielded another gun, a code-book in Russian and German, a bottle of aspirin tablets, and an ordinary three-cent pen which one can buy in any stationery store.

While Steve drove, Dan called out to him the result of his search, enumerating the objects. Suddenly, Steve brought the car to an abrupt halt in the middle of the bridge. He snapped his fingers.

"I've got it, Dan! I've got it!"

"Got what?" Dan demanded. "The rabies?"

"Don't you see? Aspirin—and a pen!" He yanked out the blank sheet of paper with the swastika letterhead, and waved it over his shoulder.

Murdoch said, "Oh! I get it!"

They had both taken an intensive course in the F.B.I. lab during the two months previous to their vacation, in the study of secret ciphers and secret inks. They had learned the curious fact that half a tablet of aspirin, dissolved in a whiskey-jigger of water, makes an effective invisible ink. The combination of the aspirin and the pen in Madame Vorovna's handbag had caused that piece of information to click in Steve's mind.

He turned around in the seat, and grinned at her. "Your

mistake, Madame Vorovna. You shouldn't have carried the pen with you. When we get this paper in the laboratory and set it under an ultra-violet lamp for eight minutes, the writing will come up. Don't you want to tell us the secret of this paper—and save us the time?"

Madame Vorovna threw up her hands in despair. "I'm beaten," she said in a small voice. "That paper will convict me—in my own writing." She looked up at Steve. "If I tell you everything you want to know, will you promise me immunity?"

Steve shook his head. "I haven't the authority to promise immunity. I can only say that if you help us to save the Forge River plant, and to save Miss Trent's life, I'll recommend clemency."

She clenched her hands tightly. "Then I won't talk. I can tell you this—that all plans are made to destroy the plant at ten-thirty tonight, and that nothing you can do without my help will save it. The girl will die."

"So will you," said Dan. "With the way the public feels about Russia today, any jury would convict you of complicity in first degree murder. You'd go to the chair."

"That would be better than a life in jail."

Steve glanced at his watch. It was seventeen minutes after ten. Thirteen minutes to go.

"Let's go, Dan," he said grimly. "We'll do the best we can."

THE FORGE RIVER plant was on the east bank of the river, about two hundred yards from the bridge. It was a vast, sprawling conglomeration of buildings, surrounded by a barbed-wire, electrified fence. There were eight gates, with signs above them designating them as East, Northeast, West, Northwest, etc. The plant had not yet gone on night shifts, and most of the buildings were dark, but the grounds themselves were fairly well lighted by street lamps spaced at regular intervals. Inside the barbed wire fence there were paved streets and a narrow gauge track for handcars, upon which the shells were wheeled from the assembly line to the storage chambers.

Steve drove along the road which skirted the fence, and caught a glimpse of two or three armed men patrolling the grounds. All the gates were closed, but at the Northeast one he saw a man on duty with a rifle.

And in the shadow of a tree across the road from the gate, he spied the unmistakable figure of Johnny Kerrigan. He slowed up, and whistled—three long and two short.

Johnny recognized the signal, and came over to the car, out from behind the shelter of the tree. He was dragging what looked like an inert sack along the ground behind him. As he got nearer, Steve and Dan saw that it was the unconscious body of a man, dressed in the uniform of a plant guard.

Dan Murdoch opened the door of the car for him, and he slung his captive inside, climbed in after him. He looked at Madame Vorovna, and whistled.

"Hello, Baby," he said.

She dropped her eyes, and did not answer.

Dan Murdoch looked down at the unconscious guard. "What you got here, Johnny? Mackerel or halibut?"

"I don't know yet," Johnny told him. "More like a stinkfish. I followed that odd-looking gent out here, and it turned out he wasn't old at all. He came with Baby here, and she left him at the gate, and drove away hell bent for leather. Then the old gent turned his collar down and took off this glasses and raised his shoulders, and he wasn't old any more. He's a pretty husky guy. He rang the bell at the gate there, and the guard came. The funny part of it was that the guard spoke to him in—guess what?"

"In German!" Steve said from the front seat.

"Right!" said Johnny. "And the young-old gent answered in German. Then the guard opened the gate for him. I hung around, trying to figure a way to get in there, and pretty soon one of the guards came out in a hurry and passed right by where I was standing under the tree. So I bopped him, and I was just getting ready to change clothes with him and go in there, when you guys came along."

"Well," said Steve, "we've got to get in there somehow. That plant's going up in smoke in eleven minutes. You put on the uniform and get the gate open, then I'll pile the car through. That's the only chance."

"Okay," said Johnny.

Dan Murdoch's dark eyes flickered at Madame Vorovna. "And we're taking you in with us, lady. There'll be a lot of shooting, and you'll be right in the middle of it."

"Hurry up," said Steve. "We're wasting time."

Johnny started to pull his coat off.

"Wait!" Madame Vorovna whispered.

"You three men are fools," she hurried on. "Brave, idiotic fools. Don't you understand that when von Spegler plans something, it is not to be broken up by *anything?* They have taken over the plant tonight. All the regular guards are killed or prisoners. Von Spegler's men have taken their place. They have put time fuses in the shell storage chambers. Before ten-thirty they will leave by an underground passage. Any minutes now they will be gone. It will be impossible for you three to fight your way through the guards and reach the shell chambers in time to stop the explosion. You will be caught in it."

"Lady," said Dan, "we can try. Go ahead, Johnny. She's just wasting our time. Every minute counts."

She twisted her hands desperately in her lap. "Oh, oh, you fools! At least—let me stay outside."

"Sorry, lady," Murdoch told her apologetically. "You're coming with us."

JOHNNY HAD his coat off, and was stripping the uniform coat from the guard. She watched him for a second, and then she wilted.

"Wait! You cannot succeed this way. You will all be killed, and I with you. I—I give up. I—will help you!"

"All right," Stephen Klaw grated. "Talk fast. There's only eight minutes left."

"That paper—it is a secret treaty between myself, as head of Russian espionage in America, and von Spegler, as head of Nazi Secret Service here. Between us we worked out the plot to destroy these plants. You'll decipher the paper anyway, in your laboratory, so I might as well tell you now. We thought we had arranged everything through a secret emissary with this Captain Trent, whom neither of us had met. Next week, Russia is to declare war on Japan, and Germany marches into Belgium. So we planned to destroy this great American ammunition plant, and leave evidence that it was the work of Japanese agents. In that way, we hoped to force America into war with Japan, thus giving Nippon an additional enemy. While the Japanese fleet was busy engaging the American fleet, Soviet Russia would be free to attack Yokohama!"

"Nice people!" said Johnny Kerrigan.

Stephen Klaw looked at his watch.

"Keep talking. And get to the point. There's seven and a half minutes left. Don't think you can talk us out of this. We're going in—even if we only have one minute left."

"Yes, yes. I believe you. Listen carefully. Von Spegler waits only for me to return, with the shell containing the secret treaty. We could not afford to let that fall into American hands. We tried every means of getting it from you. Von Spegler even posed as Captain Trent, but you did not believe him. You sent him after me, on a wild goose chase. We were sure you would not escape Venic and his men, in your room, but you beat us there, too. Luckily, the girl, Nancy Trent, came here to the gate. Our men spotted her, and captured her. She is a prisoner in there, and von Spegler sent me to bargain with you for her life, in the remote event that you escaped from Venic."

"Skip all the rest," Steve warned her, "and get down to your plan. You said you'd help us get in."

"Yes. Let Murdoch and Kerrigan hide on the floor of the car. You will drive me to the gate. I will say that you have come to speak to von Spegler personally. They will let us in. Once you are inside the gates, you will drive the car toward that first building, where the lights are on. You, Stephen Klaw, will come inside with me. Kerrigan and Murdoch will wait until the guards are gone back to their posts. Then they will follow. Von Spegler has the detonators in that building. I—"

The words were jarred out of her as Steve sent the car hurtling forward toward the northeast gate.

"We're off, Mopes!" he shouted. "Get down on your bellies!"

Dan and Johnny just had time to crouch on the floor with the unconscious guard before Steve brought the car to a screeching halt, with the headlights almost touching the gate.

Two guards with automatic rifles came running forward, peering through the gate bars.

Madame Vorovna leaned out of the window, while Dan Murdoch, crouching on the floor just behind her, held a gun against her ribs.

"Remember, lady," he whispered, "this is no time to pull any fast ones!" He could feel her body pulsing.

She was thoroughly cowed. She spoke swiftly in German to the guard, and Dan Murdoch, who spoke the language like a native, was satisfied. She was telling the man that she had brought someone to speak with von Spegler.

The guard glanced suspiciously at Steve, and said something about having to ask his superiors. But she spat at him viciously that he was a fool. Didn't he know there was no time. In a minute or two they must all leave here, before the explosion.

"Open quickly, dolt!" she ordered, her eyes snapping.

The man was more responsive to abuse than he might have been to kind words and coaxing. He was used to obeying orders, and he knew that she was working with his master. He nodded to his companion, and they removed the bar from the gate, swung it open.

STEVE BARELY waited until the two wings of the gate were all the way back. His watch showed nearly twenty-five minutes after ten. Already they could see a small group of figures coming out of the lighted building, and hurrying away toward the north end of the grounds. Those were the first of the saboteurs to leave. Shortly, von Spegler, too, would be making his escape, leaving the plant mined, and set with the time-detonators.

Steve spurred the car ahead, barely clearing the opening wings of the gate, and roared in first, straight across the grounds to the door of the big white building. Above the entrance was a sign reading:

SHELL STORAGE CHAMBER NUMBER ONE

Steve stepped hard on the brake, and the car narrowly escaped running down a group of men who were coming out of the building. They muttered oaths in German, but did not stop. They had no reason to believe that this car was occupied by other than Madame Vorovna, for they had seen her in it before.

Steve watched them, with his hands on his automatics, while Dan and Johnny crouched out of sight.

Madame Vorovna said, "Those are the last of von Spegler's men. He has given the order to clear out. He will be in there with only a half-dozen more, at the most."

John Kerrigan, peering over the side of the car, growled, "Should we let these mutts get away? Let's open up on them!"

"Nix!" Steve said hurriedly. "Let them go. The fewer we have to battle with, the better."

They let another whole, precious minute elapse, until that last group had moved down the path toward the north gate. Then Steve opened the door and got out. He walked around the car, and Madame Vorovna put her hand on the handle of her door.

"I will take you up to him."

"Don't bother, Madame Vorovna," Steve said drily. "From here on, we can find our way by ourselves."

She looked suddenly frightened. "What—what are you going to do with me?"

"Just keep you safe, lady," Dan Murdoch said softly. "I hope you don't mind."

He drew her two wrists behind her, and Johnny Kerrigan got the belt off the unconscious guard. They fixed the belt tightly around her wrists, and then Dan used two handkerchiefs for a gag.

They stepped out of the car, leaving her on the seat, with her shapely legs resting on the inert body of the guard.

"It's much better this way," Steve told her. "You won't be in the line of fire. And you won't be tempted to double-cross us at the last minute."

He swung around toward the entrance and Kerrigan and Murdoch stepped to either side of him. Then, shoulder to shoulder, Kerrigan and Murdoch and Klaw went into Shell Chamber Number One.

CHAPTER 8
AN ACRE OF DESTRUCTION

JUST INSIDE the entrance there was a small enclosure, wired in, with a door leading into the storage space. A big sign said:

NO SMOKING!
Penalty for violation of this Rule:
One Year in Prison or $500 fine, or Both!
This Law Is Strictly Enforced!

Another sign read:

At the First Sound of the Fire Alarm Gong, All Persons Will
Make for the Nearest Exit Without Delay!

"It looks like they're afraid of fire," Johnny Kerrigan said, lighting a cigarette.

He kept the cigarette in his mouth, and took out his two revolvers. Dan Murdoch already had his out. Stephen Klaw had both hands in his pockets.

The door in the wired partition was open, and they stepped through. There was a short corridor, with a private office on the left. Steve peered in, but saw no one. He nodded to Johnny and Dan, and the three of them moved on.

At the end of the corridor, they stepped out into the immense shell storage chamber.

"My Gawd!" Johnny breathed, around the cigarette between

his lips. "Imagine these things exploding all at once. They'd make a hole all the way to China!"

"They'd make a hole in you, too, lug!" Dan Murdoch whispered. "Why don't you kill that butt!"

"Nix!" grinned Johnny. "This may be my last smoke. I aim to enjoy it to the last puff."

The immense floor spread in front of them, occupying almost an acre of space. And it was completely filled with finished shells, standing row upon row, towering above all three of them—huge monsters of destruction, made of steel and powder, containing enough combined destructive force to bury a dozen great cities in an avalanche of ruin and debris.

"No wonder they keep a plant like this on the other side of the river!" said Dan Murdoch. His voice was strained.

"Ps-st!" whispered Steve. "There they are!"

Their eyes followed his pointing automatic. A small group of men was clustered about one of the shells.

Stephen Klaw recognized von Spegler among them. He was the one who had talked to him in the hotel, telling him the fairy story about having concealed a time-bomb in the shell. The man was changed, but he still had that little scar on the side of his chin. Steve noticed it as von Spegler arose from something he had been doing at the shell.

When they saw what it was that von Spegler had been doing, they drew in their breath sharply.

Nancy Trent was tied to that shell! And von Spegler had just finished lighting a three-inch fuse set into a hole in the shell's casing!

SHELLS FOR THE SUICIDE SQUAD

The German spymaster blew out the match carefully, and chuckled. The six men around him laughed uproariously. Nancy Trent, bound to the shell, stood with her chin up, her lips bravely compressed.

Von Spegler bowed to her. "And now, my dear, we shall leave you. In exactly four minutes, the fuse will burn down to the casing."

He gestured toward the sputtering fuse. "I trust that the subsequent fireworks will be to your liking."

Nancy Trent stared at him with loathing. "You devil!" she breathed. "You dirty devil!"

Von Spegler shrugged. "It is the fortune of war, my dear. You see, it's out of the question for us to leave you alive. You know too much for our comfort. It is too bad that your brother took you into his confidence tonight, before he died. A scientist should never engage in international intrigue. He should have stuck to his chemistry instead of trying to trap us by pretending to sell us the shell model."

Nancy Trent flared at him, "Your agent poisoned Paul! You beast, you ordered him murdered!"

"Quite so," von Spegler said complacently. "Your brother was the only army chemist who was familiar with the process of manufacturing the explosive for this new shell. Now, after we destroy this plant, the United States will be unable to supply them to our enemies."

He glanced at the sputtering fuse, and frowned. "Two minutes more to go. We have ample time. The plane at the other side of the building will take us all away before the explosion. I would like to ask you a question, though. Before you die, Miss Trent, wouldn't you like to tell me the identity of those three fire-eaters—the one who posed as your brother, and the other two who shoot like inhuman devils?"

"Yes," said Nancy. "I'll tell you. They're the Suicide Squad. And I can face death, you beast, because I know they'll get you. When my brother found the secret treaty that your messenger dropped, he knew he was doomed. He put it in the shell and gave it to me. And I phoned Washington for help. Venic and Mueller kept close watch on me, but I managed to phone when I went to the ladies' room. I had to get that treaty into the hands of an American agent. And now, von Spegler, Stephen Klaw has it. He'll find you—he and his two partners—and he'll kill you!"

Von Spegler laughed. "I shall be out of the country in two hours, my dear. And my very capable assistants will recover the treaty from Klaw. In fact, I shouldn't wonder if those three are already dead—"

Kerrigan and Murdoch and Klaw had been listening, and watching the burning fuse. Klaw whispered, "I guess we've heard enough, eh?"

Johnny and Dan nodded grimly.

Steve took out both his automatics and snicked off the safety catches.

Von Spegler was finishing: "—if those three are not already dead, they soon will—"

Stephen Klaw interrupted him, drawling, "I'm sorry, *Herr* von Spegler, but you're just a bit too optimistic!"

THE GERMAN spymaster spat out an oath, and swung

around. The six men with him uttered guttural shouts. Guns appeared in their hands.

Down the aisle, came Kerrigan and Murdoch and Klaw, side by side, guns spouting swift and sure death. Down that aisle, flanked on either side by huge shells each containing a half ton of explosive, the Suicide Squad marched. They fired coolly, carefully, so as not to hit a shell. But they moved ever forward.

Von Spegler and the others answered their fire, but they shot gingerly, nervously, knowing that one stray bullet would send the whole place up into Kingdom Come, with them in it.

The blasting, thunderous detonations of the heavy guns filled the great storage chamber, the echoes rolling back to them in beating waves of sound.

Two, three of the enemy were down. Dan Murdoch jerked upright with a bullet in the hip. Steve Klaw took one along his ribs. But neither of them stopped. They kept moving forward and shooting as they came, and two more of the spies died. Only *Herr* von Spegler remained on his feet. His eyes were bugging out.

The fuse was sputtering down to the shell casing. Nancy Trent stared wide-eyed at the deadly battle in front of her, while total destruction burned at the end of that fuse, only a few inches from her waist.

Von Spegler, his face white, turned to run down the aisle of shells, wildly, in panic. Johnny Kerrigan stopped shooting and sprang over to the shell where Nancy was tied, grabbed at the burning fuse with his bare fingers and yanked it out of the shell casing. He let out a thick grunt as fire bit into his fingers.

But Steve and Dan didn't stop shooting. Grimly, deliberately, they sent their slugs after the madly fleeing man. They lowered their sights, and cut the German's legs from under him with a burst that shook the vast room.

Von Spegler uttered a despairing cry as he fell to the floor. A spasm of hate and rage crossed his face. He raised his gun and aimed it at the nearest shell. He would have to face the American electric chair if he lived. He might as well go out this way. They heard him muttering to himself in German.

His finger tightened on the trigger and he screamed, *"Die, American pigs!"* Saliva drooled from his mouth.

But he never fired. Dan Murdoch, with a sigh of reluctance, shot him through the head. The G-man watched as his face became a bloody lather.

Johnny Kerrigan had cut Nancy Trent free of the shell, and he led her over to Dan and Steve. They were both bleeding, but they had been wounded often enough in the past to know when a wound was serious and when it wasn't. They grinned at Nancy, and Steve said, "Hello, sister." Then he stopped grinning.

She was crying softly. "You—you must think me an awful baby," she gulped, her eyes silvered with tears.

"No, Nancy," Steve told her softly. "You're tops with us. With all three of us. I never saw a girl who could face death the way you just did. You have a right to cry."

"Th-thank you," she mumbled, and buried her head against his shoulder, her body trembling.

He led her out to the yard, with Johnny and Dan preceding them. The cool air of the night felt good on fevered skin.

Outside, there were a dozen police cars, with spotlights turned onto the ground. The guards had opened the gates and raised their hands in token of surrender. The police swarmed in, overwhelming Kerrigan and Murdoch and Klaw with their congratulations. The G-men tried to get out, but to no avail.

It was more than an hour before they, could get away. At last, after having their wounds treated and seeing the escaped spies rounded up, they bundled Nancy Trent into the limousine, and Johnny drove out of the grounds, past the spotlights whipping over the yard.

Across the bridge, Johnny stopped. Steve bent down and untied the wrists of Madame Vorovna, who was still lying on the floor of the car. They had unloaded the unconscious guard, but they had said nothing to the police about their feminine captive. Steve took off her gag and looked at her.

She chafed her wrists, looking from them to Nancy Trent. "Well," she said, "what are you going to do with me?" Her eyes were dull.

"Nothing," Steve told her. "Here's your bag. I see it has plenty of money in it. Get out of the country if you can. Without your help, we wouldn't have been able to stop von Spegler. We're giving you a break. I hate to do it, but you did play square with us."

For a long minute she was silent, her breasts heaving with some strange emotion. Then she said huskily, "Thank you, Kerrigan and Murdoch and Klaw. In my business, the quality of mercy is unknown. It—it is strange to me. I do not know what to say. But I shall always remember. Some day, perhaps, I may be able to repay you three. Someday, I may meet you three again."

She leaned forward suddenly and kissed Stephen Klaw full on the lips. Then she got out of the car and walked swiftly away into the darkness—walked until the night swallowed her in its blanket of ebony mist.

Nancy Trent looked after her with taut, drawn features. "Why does the world have to be so terrible!" she cried. "Why must nations fight and plot against other nations, and warp the lives of men and women!" She sobbed suddenly and her breasts heaved.

Dan Murdoch pressed her hand. "It's the nature of the world, Nancy, and it'll never change. As long as the world goes on there will be war, and a struggle among the races of man for mastery. The desire for power and glory makes the world go on. Without it, there would be no incentive for progress. The tragedy is that the same ambitions which bring progress to the earth must also bring destruction." Murdoch lapsed into a silence that lasted a long time.

Nancy shook her head. "Think of the lives that were lost tonight. Paul. Von Spegler. Venic. All those poor tools of Von Spegler's—"

"And not forgetting the bravest of all!" Stephen Klaw broke in. "Let's go and get your bottle of Highland Sabre, Dan. We've got to drink a toast to a man—Lieutenant Suzuke Inyo—who knew how to die with a smile!"

Then the three men and the girl drove into the night.

THE SUICIDE SQUAD'S
MURDER LOTTERY

CHAPTER 1
A G-MAN FOR THE MORGUE

D AN MURDOCH was without doubt the handsomest of that trio of daredevil hellions who were known as the F.B.I. Suicide Squad. Dark-haired, tall and supple, he was the one whom the ladies admired most when pictures of the Suicide Squad appeared in the newspapers.

Not that he permitted his looks to interfere with the quality of his marksmanship. On the pistol range, neither Kerrigan nor Klaw could beat his record. In fact, those three ran so close together that they had given up trying to compete with one another.

But tonight, Dan Murdoch was enjoying a distinct advantage over his two partners, due to the fact that he was "tall, dark and handsome." He was in Silverton, on the most dangerous end of an assignment, while Johnny Kerrigan was in Cleveland and Stephen Klaw in Cincinnati, both bored stiff on dead-end angles of the same case.

The way it came about was that Martha Gray had written a letter addressed to Dan Murdoch, saying that she had seen his picture in the papers last month, and that if he would come to see her in the place where she was hiding out in Silverton, she

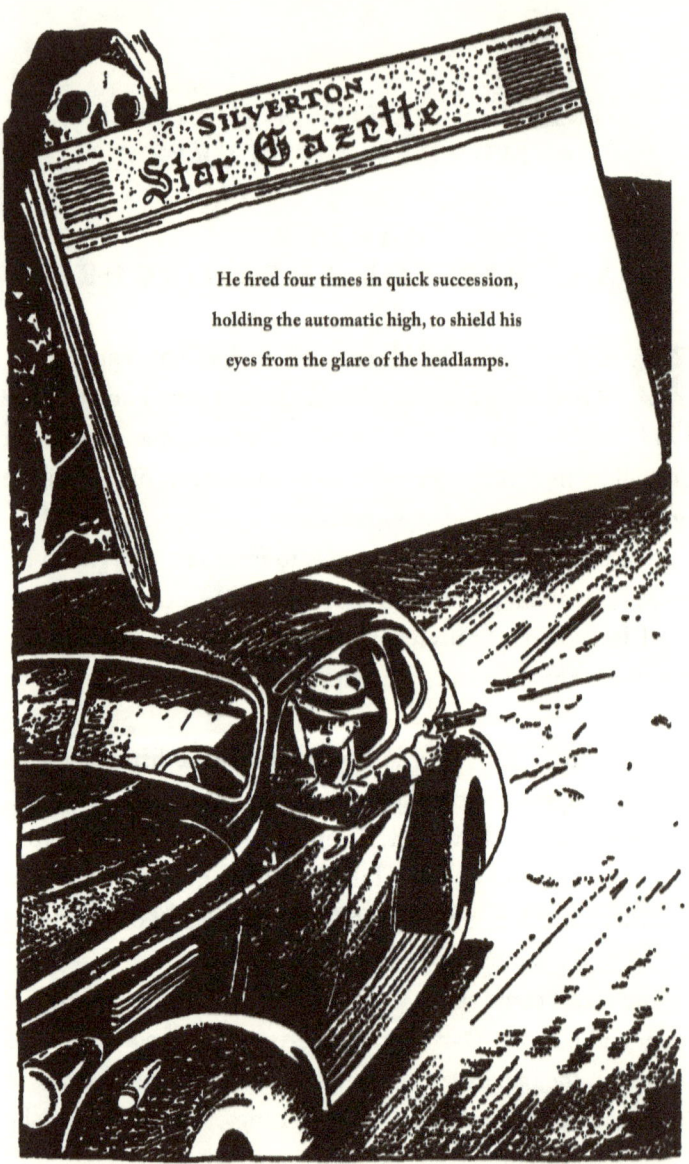

SILVERTON
Star Gazette

He fired four times in quick succession,
holding the automatic high, to shield his
eyes from the glare of the headlamps.

would give him information that would help him to break the power of Nicholas Lafflin's immense crime empire.

The pictures of Kerrigan and Klaw had been printed in the newspapers at the same time, with accounts of their successful thwarting of the sabotage plans of the Nazi-Russian spy-ring headed by the notorious Von Spegler. But it was

Murdoch's photograph which had drawn the letter. So here he was in Silverton, laughing up his sleeve at Johnny and Steve.

He knew he was being followed, the moment he stepped off the train. A man with a bulbous nose, who had sat across the aisle all the way from Washington, got into the cab directly behind his. To confirm his suspicion that Bulbous-nose was interested in following him, Dan told his driver not to start at once, but to wait a minute or two. Sure enough, the cab behind, which had started already, pulled over to the curb farther down the block, and waited.

Dan grinned to himself. He tapped on the window and said, "Drive slowly, and go through the Silverton Park. There'll be a cab following us."

"Want me to lose 'em, mister?" the cabby asked.

"On the contrary," Dan said softly. "I want to make sure we *don't* lose them. I have a few words to say to that gentleman—when we get some privacy."

"Look, mister," said the cabby. "I'm an honest man."

"So am I," Dan told him, showing him his F.B.I. badge.

"That's different!" the other grinned. "Let's go!"

He sent the cab ahead slowly, and turned west toward the Park. Bulbous-nose's cab tailed them, about fifty feet behind.

Dan Murdoch figured he had the situation well under control. But there was one thing he didn't know—that a convertible cabriolet, with the top up, was following the second cab, another fifty feet behind. And that a man with a sawed-off shotgun sat next to the driver of that convertible, while another man with a sub-machine gun was crouching in the rear.

IT WAS only when they were well into the Park, in a fairly secluded and dark section, that Murdoch found out about the cabriolet. His intention was to stop Bulbous-nose's cab, a little farther on, and have a heart-to-heart talk with him.

There was no doubt in Dan's mind that Bulbous-nose was an agent of Duke Lafflin, the infamous newspaper publisher whose sixty-odd papers all over the country were only a screed for an immense lottery racket. Lafflin would be very anxious to locate Martha Gray and silence her before she could talk. The best way to do that, naturally, was to follow Dan Murdoch. But Dan's idea was to turn the tables and put the screws on Bulbous-nose, in an effort to make him spill some information that would incriminate Lafflin.

Dan was just about to lean forward and instruct his own cabby to slow up when he became aware of a fresh set of head-lights sweeping on from behind, in addition to those of Bulbous-nose's cab.

He twisted around in his seat, and saw the convertible, gunning forward to pass the taxicab. Bulbous-nose was lean-ing out and pointing at Murdoch's cab. Then, as the cab's lights splashed across the convertible, Murdoch saw the man with the sawed-off shotgun.

There were only about ten seconds to spare before that car would come abreast of them. A glint of satisfaction came into Murdoch's eyes. It was said of Kerrigan and Murdoch and Klaw, that no three Federal agents who had ever worked together were as much alike in their pursuit of danger, and their enjoyment of deadly battle. There was good reason for the nickname of the

Suicide Squad. They got only those assignments from which there was little chance of returning alive. That was the way they wanted it.

If Duke Lafflin knew that the Suicide Squad was after him, and those men in the convertible were Lafflin's hirelings, they would start blasting at once. They wouldn't take any chances. In those few seconds before they came abreast of him, Murdoch's only thought was for his own cab driver, who was only an innocent party to the whole thing, but who surely would be killed, together with himself, in the first blast.

The driver had sensed what was coming, and was frantically swinging his cab over to the right side of the road, in a panicky effort to get away.

Dan Murdoch yanked open the door on the left hand side of the cab, and leaped out to the pavement, in this way he hoped to draw the fire from the cabriolet away from his driver. Two heavy service revolvers appeared in his hands, and he stood spraddle-legged alongside the now-halted cab, sending twin streams of slugs into the speeding convertible.

His first slug took the man with the shotgun squarely in the chest, smashing him back against the driver, who tried to shove the dead body aside and at the same time keep the wheel steady. The muzzle of a machine gun appeared in the rear window, in the hands of a man crouched behind the driver's seat. Murdoch emptied both his guns into the rear aperture. He saw the first blast of lead pour from the machine gun, and go wild. Then the deadly muzzle dropped from the inert hands of the gunner, and the cabriolet sped away with roaring motor.

Dan Murdoch laughed out loud. "Score one for the weak side!" he said to his cabby, who came scrambling out of the cab, with quaking knees.

Then he swung toward Bulbous-nose's cab. It had come to a stop, and its driver had tumbled out and disappeared into the woods at a dead run. He wanted no part of this gunfight.

Bulbous-nose was scrambling around to get in under the wheel and escape, when Dan Murdoch came running over, with both empty guns in his hands. Dan poked one of the unloaded weapons into Bulbous-nose's side.

"Shall I pull the trigger?" he asked sweetly. "Or do you cross your arms over your chest?"

BULBOUS-NOSE GASPED, and quickly crossed his arms over his chest. If he had bothered to count the flashes from Murdoch's guns, he would have known that there was nothing lethal in them now. But he wasn't interested. All he knew was that this man, whose revolvers had beaten a machine gun, was telling him to do something. And he was eager to do it—before Murdoch got really angry.

Dan grinned. He grabbed Bulbous-nose by the collar, and shoved him in under the wheel.

"I think I'll use your cab for the rest of the night," he said. "And *you'll* drive!"

"W-whatever you s-say!" Bulbous-nose stuttered.

Murdoch called over his own driver, and gave him twenty dollars. "It goes on the F.B.I. expense account, so don't worry about it. Anyway, you earned it."

He watched the man get in the other cab and drive away, and then climbed in the rear of his new taxi.

"You may drive on, James," he said. "Straight ahead, the same way that convertible went."

Bulbous-nose was so nervous he could barely keep the wheel steady. "They'll be w-waiting at the Park exit." he stammered. "They'll t-try again."

"What's your name?" Murdoch demanded.

"Hulick. I—"

"You work for Lafflin?"

"So help me, mister, I don't know who I work for. I—I got a number—C-54. All I know is, I take orders from another agent, a dame, and her number is B-70. She gets orders from someone else, I don't know who. Believe me, mister, I don't know a thing!"

"I haven't started asking you yet," Murdoch said softly. "You'll remember a lot, all right—when I start asking!"

Murdoch had finished reloading his guns by the time they reached the Park exit. Sure enough, there was the convertible cabriolet, parked at the curb across the Circle. It started moving as soon as they appeared.

There was a lot of traffic on the Circle, and its rumble almost drowned out the querulous voice of Hulick as he said over his shoulder, "They're gonna try again, mister. For God's sake, lemme outta here!"

But Hulick was talking to thin air. Dan Murdoch had quietly opened the door of the cab, and stepped out on the far side, as they slowed down for traffic. He closed the door gently, and strode quickly over to the curb, mingling with the crowd.

He looked over his shoulder. The convertible cabriolet had made a wide U turn, disregarding the oncoming traffic, and was now drawing alongside the cab. They must have picked up reinforcements here at the Circle, for two sub-machine guns were poked out of the windows, and a concentrated blast of fire was directed at the cab. Slowly, the convertible pulled past the cab, while the gunners inside raked it, fore and aft. They made certain no one could remain alive, and then pulled away.

Hulick slumped over the wheel, and the cab veered over and collided with a car in the next lane of traffic. Soon a crowd was gathered around it.

MURDOCH JOINED the crowd. Hulick's body was riddled with bullets, and one of the bursts had carried away most of his face. In the confusion, several people dragged him out onto the pavement, thinking there was a chance to save his life, but when they saw his face they gave up.

The police, who arrived in a few minutes, thought that Hulick had been a passenger in the cab. Murdoch, listening, did not disillusion them. He watched them go through the dead man's pockets. They found nothing. Apparently, the agents of Duke Lafflin were instructed to rid themselves of all identification when they went out on a job.

Dan Murdoch got an idea. He fished some unimportant letters and a telegram out of his pockets; most of them bore his own name. Swiftly, he stooped and rubbed them around in the dirt and blood on the ground, and then called in a loud voice, "Here, Officer! Here's some papers that must have fallen out of his coat."

The police grabbed them, not even casting a second glance at Murdoch, and began to examine them eagerly. From their faces, it was evident to Dan that they were looking for a certain thing. And they found it. With a grunt of satisfaction, a police captain who had been addressed as Captain Draper, pointed to the name of Dan Murdoch on the letters.

"It's him, all right," he said to another policeman. "It's Murdoch, the G-man. They got him, after all."

There was a very smug and satisfied expression on Captain Draper's countenance as he carefully put the papers away, and directed the removal of "Murdoch's" body to the Morgue.

Dan Murdoch flicked an invisible speck from the lapel of his coat, and turned away. In a few moments he was out of the Circle, and in another cab. He drove to the east side of the city, and then walked four blocks. Now he was only a block from the address which Martha Gray had given in her letter.

With an appearance of casualness, he eyed the street. At least two of the men he saw loitering along the block looked as if they had been posted there for a purpose. One of them leaned negligently against the doorway of a candy store, another was pacing up and down alongside a parked car, and smoking a cigar, examining everyone who came out of the building in front of which he stood. This block consisted of a row of four apartment houses on one side, and a row of two-family brick houses on the other.

Martha Gray was holed up in Number Fourteen, the second of the apartment houses. She had written in her letter that Lafflin's watchers knew she was somewhere in this block, that they were watching everyone who came out, and that she had no chance of evading them. Murdoch saw that she had been right. The only thing Lafflin's agents didn't know, was which apartment she was in.

He couldn't take the chance of going boldly in, past the watchers. They might recognize him. As far as he himself was concerned, he didn't mind attracting their attention. But he had no right to lead them to Martha Gray's hideout.

HIS GLANCE swept up the street, and settled on a fire box at the corner. His eyes glinted. He sauntered past the fire box, looked around to make sure no one was watching him, and broke the glass with the little hammer hanging alongside by a chain. Then he reached in swiftly and pulled the lever.

In less than four minutes, red-painted engines were clanging into the street, and the men in white rubber coats were swarming all over, looking for the fire. Everyone, including the gunmen, turned to watch the excitement. And Dan Murdoch stole swiftly into Number Fourteen, unobserved.

It was a walk-up flat. He hurried up the three flights to the top floor. He rapped three times on the door of Apartment 4A, then four times, then twice, then three times again. This was the complicated signal Martha Gray had given in her letter.

Almost as if she had been waiting for the signal with her hand on the knob, the door came open. Murdoch smiled at the young woman who stood there. She looked terrified, with one hand at her breast, the other holding a revolver. The revolver was wobbling all over the place, and she would have been certain to hit anything but the person she aimed at.

Dan Murdoch showed her his badge, and stepped inside.

He patted Martha Gray on the shoulder, took the gun out of her hand.

"You can put that away now, Martha," he told her gently. "The Marines have arrived."

He closed and locked the door, and when he turned around to face her, she began to sob silently. Like a trusting child, she buried her head against his shoulder, crying frankly, without shame.

"That's it, girlie. Cry," Dan said.

After a moment, she stopped. She looked up at him, without drying her eyes, and he saw that she was very pretty. Even the strain of being hunted by Duke Lafflin's ruthless organization had not detracted from her loveliness.

"I shouldn't have sent for you!" she said. "I've—only brought you to your death. We'll never get out of this house alive. Even you—couldn't get me past those killers outside!"

"Those guys aren't as tough as they look, Martha. If you have information that will help to convict Duke Lafflin, I'll see that you get into court to testify."

"But—but you can't shoot your way out through them all— with me!"

"Well, no. But I can go out and phone Washington. I've got a couple of pals who'll be here tomorrow—"

"You can't! You can't do that! I know. They follow every stranger who comes out of these houses. They've been here a week, and they know all the regular faces. If they saw you go out now, they'd follow you till they found out who you were. And if you went to use a phone, they'd shoot you down!"

"H—m!" said Dan. "Lafflin is pretty thorough, isn't he?"

"More thorough than you suspect," she said bitterly. "I don't know why I sent for you. I—I should have given up. It's no use fighting Lafflin."

"We'll see about that," Murdoch said grimly.

CHAPTER 2
DEN OF THE DUKE

NICHOLAS DUDLEY LAFFLIN—known throughout the newspaper world as Duke Lafflin—reached out a well-kept, well-manicured hand, and selected a custom-made cigar from the onyx-and-silver humidor upon his desk. The band around the cigar was embellished with a coat-of-arms surmounted by a gold crown. Beneath the gaudy emblem appeared the initials 'N. D. L.'

His secretary, Armand Taussig, came up with alacrity from a chair beside the desk, and held a lighter for him. Momentarily, the purple flame of the lighter illuminated the hawk-nosed, predatory countenance of the great publisher in a luminosity that seemed almost evil.

Lafflin puffed the cigar to a glow and sank back in his chair.

Armand Taussig withdrew the lighter, replaced it on the desk. "Thank you, sir," he said. He stood stiffly erect, his spine like a ramrod.

Nicholas Dudley Lafflin leaned back with the cigar between his thin, ruthless lips, and allowed his eyes to survey the office.

Covering one entire wall was a big map of the United States.

93

There were sixty-four small pins stuck in the map, and each pin had a red enameled head. They were in sixty-four of the most important cities of the country, and each one represented a Lafflin-owned newspaper.

In addition to those, there were other pins—some green, some yellow, some black. Nobody except Lafflin and Armand Taussig knew the meaning of those other pins.

Around the other walls, were portraits—of the Emperor Nero, of Napoleon Bonaparte, Julius Caesar, Adolf Hitler, Benito Mussolini and Joseph Stalin. Nicholas Dudley Lafflin's eyes came to rest on the picture of Nero. A slight, twisted smile played upon his bloodless lips. He allowed a thin trickle of aromatic smoke to curl upward from the cigar.

One of the four telephones on Armand Taussig's desk rang with a little, muted peal. Taussig said, "Excuse me, sir," and went over to the desk. He picked up the phone and said, "Well?"

He listened for a moment, then said into the instrument, "Wait!" He put down the phone and turned to Lafflin. "It is B-16, reporting from Cleveland, sir. B-16 says that our paper there, the *Cleveland Star-Herald*, has lost more than a thousand circulation a day in the last month. It is not the fault of the *Star-Herald's* manager. It's due to the fact that the rival paper, the *Cleveland Eagle*, has been taking readers away from us by hiring high-priced feature writers."

Lafflin listened with narrowed eyes. "Buy the *Cleveland Eagle*," he said laconically.

Taussig shook his head. "B-16 tried to buy it, but they wouldn't sell. He offered them a million dollars. They claim their paper is worth more than two million."

Lafflin's cold, hard face did not change its expression. "Very well," he ordered. "Destroy the *Cleveland Eagle!*"

Taussig bowed. He picked up the phone again. "You are authorized to take action along the lines of Plan Four," he said. "That is all, B-16."

HE HUNG up and came back to the larger desk. He began to read to his employer from a set of report sheets. "The net figures are as follows, sir. Last month we lost eight hundred thousand dollars on the publication of our sixty-four papers. But we made one million seven hundred thousand dollars on our—er—other operations. Leaving a net profit of nine hundred thousand dollars."

"Not enough," Lafflin said coldly. "We must increase our other operations. Instruct A-3 to recruit additional agents in other cities. Let me see...." He arose and went over to the wall map. "Let me see. We have fifteen green, or A agents, two hundred yellow, or B agents, and nine hundred black, or C agents. Our A agents must recruit another hundred B agents, who will in turn enlist five hundred more blacks. That will permit us to extend our operations to at least fifty more towns. It should raise our net profits by fifty percent."

"But, sir," Taussig interrupted, "isn't that going at it a little too strong? The F.B.I. is already beginning to notice. They're going a little easy at first, because of all the important people involved. But if we spread out, they're sure to stumble on something—"

"Bah!" exclaimed Lafflin impatiently. "Nobody can touch me.

I am too powerful. The F.B.I. can be handled—like any other organization. They're only human."

Taussig looked a little doubtful. "At least a dozen of their men have already had to be done away with, in different cities, sir. I understand they've assigned that infernal trio—the Suicide Squad—to investigate further."

Lafflin uttered a short, barking laugh. "The Suicide Squad, eh! Nothing pleases me better. Those three reckless fools will be easier to dispose of than any others. Everybody knows they take wild chances, and nobody will be surprised if they meet an untimely end. Are you following their movements?"

"Yes, sir." Armand Taussig picked up some pink sheets from his desk. "Their names are Kerrigan, Murdoch and Klaw, sir, as you know. Kerrigan has gone to Cleveland, Klaw to Cincinnati, and Murdoch to Silverton. Murdoch's task was to find Martha Gray, and convince her that she should talk."

"Martha Gray! Is she still alive?" Lafflin turned an angry glance at his secretary. "Didn't I give orders a month ago that she was to be put out of the way?"

Taussig quailed before that look. "I—I'm sorry, sir. I set twenty men on the job of finding her, but she seems to have gone to cover. They know she's in Silverton, and they're searching the city. But she must have communicated with the F.B.I. in some way, for Murdoch was going to see her. I—I took the liberty of ordering Murdoch killed—"

"Fool!" Lafflin thundered. "Why didn't you let Murdoch lead you to Martha Gray? Damn you, you've bungled this completely. Murdoch is not to be killed! See to it that he is followed and—"

One of the phones rang, and Taussig picked it up. He listened for a moment, and his face went white. He licked his lips, and covered the mouthpiece. "It—it's B-70 from Silverton, sir. He—she reports that my orders have been carried out. Dan Murdoch is dead. His body is in the Silverton Morgue."

Lafflin's anger was so great that he bit the cigar clean in two. But in a moment he controlled himself. "If Murdoch has been killed, then Kerrigan and Klaw will surely go to Silverton. We must make the most of it. Concentrate all available agents in Silverton. Put the screws on those city officials we control. See to it that neither Kerrigan nor Klaw leave Silverton alive. And, above all, Martha Gray must be found and destroyed!"

"Y-yes, sir," Taussig said. He put his mouth close to the mouthpiece, and began to issue swift orders to B-70 in Silverton....

CHAPTER 3
DEATH FLIPS A COIN

STEPHEN KLAW and Johnny Kerrigan arrived at the Silverton City Morgue at almost the same time. Kerrigan had had the greater distance to come, from Cleveland, so he had flown and taken a cab from the airport. Steve Klaw had driven over from Cincinnati in an F.B.I. car. He parked opposite the Morgue, and turned out his headlights. In less than two minutes, he saw Kerrigan descend from the cab down the block, blinked his lights twice, quickly, and Johnny came right over.

There was something ominous and terrible in the swing of

those big stevedore shoulders of Kerrigan's, and in the tightness of his bronzed features. Similarly, there was a cold and foreboding glint in the slate-grey eyes of Stephen Klaw.

There was no jubilant greeting between these two, tonight. Instead, when Johnny got into the car, he said in a hushed voice. "Steve, it can't be true, can it? God! They couldn't have got Dan that easy!"

Klaw's hands were white on the steering wheel. "The newspaper item said they found positive identification on him, Johnny. Papers with his name on them—and letters."

"But not his badge, Steve," Kerrigan reminded slowly. "Not his badge."

For a minute they both sat silent. Then Stephen Klaw stirred. "I'll go in and look at the body, Johnny."

"Better let me go in," Kerrigan said.

They turned and looked at each other. Each knew what was in the other's mind. The same powerful forces which had attacked Dan Murdoch would be waiting for Kerrigan and Klaw to appear. Those forces would never be content, would never feel safe, until Johnny Kerrigan and Stephen Klaw were also wiped out. It would be inviting death to go openly to the Morgue and ask to see Murdoch's body.

Without a word, Stephen Klaw took out a silver dollar. Kerrigan nodded. Klaw flipped the heavy coin in the air, caught it in his left hand, and smacked it down on the back of his right.

"Heads!" said Johnny Kerrigan.

Steve uncovered the silver dollar. It was tails.

Steve smiled faintly. Johnny Kerrigan scowled. "All right,

Shrimp, you win. Go on in. But if you don't come out in twenty minutes, I'm going in there and tear the damned place wide apart!"

"Make it a half hour," Steve said.

He opened the door of the car, and stepped out. Kerrigan moved over under the wheel.

"Keep the motor running, Johnny," Steve said. "I may be coming out in a hurry."

Kerrigan only nodded.

Steve thrust both hands in his jacket pockets, and started across the street.

"So long, Mope!" he said in a forced voice.

"So long, Shrimp! Keep your ears dry!" Kerrigan called after him, with an effort at joviality.

STEVE WAS halfway across the street when the powerful headlights of an automobile, parked down the street, splashed their high beams up the length of the block, silhouetting Steve between them. Gears clashed, and a motor roared under the pressure of swift acceleration. The car came speeding up the street like a streak of lightning, bearing straight for Stephen Klaw.

As it passed under a street lamp it was revealed as a newspaper truck, with high sides plastered with posters advertising the *Silverton Star-Gazette.* It veered a bit to the left, so as to catch Klaw before he could reach the curb. The man at the wheel was distinctly visible, hunched forward, his face a cold mask of murderous intent.

As it bore down on Stephen Klaw, a second man swung out

on the running board, cradling a sub-machine gun under his arm. He clung to the windshield frame with one arm, and raised his ugly-snouted weapon, lining it on Klaw.

They were making sure to get him—one way or another. There was no way to avoid that man-guided projectile, nor even to escape the hail of lead which would pour from the machine gun in another half-second. Even if Klaw should turn to run— which was farthest from his thoughts—the truck would smash into him before he could hope to reach cover. And failing that, the machine gun would surely cut him down.

Klaw stopped short, and swung to face the hurtling double doom. His right hand came out of his jacket pocket, gripping a flat, black automatic. But he was blinded by the headlamps. He could see the bulk of the machine gunner on the running board, but he could not see where to place an effective shot that might stop the speeding truck.

Nevertheless, Stephen Klaw held his ground. Upon his lips was that same faint smile which had been there when he had won the toss from Johnny Kerrigan.

He fired four times in quick succession, holding the automatic high, and to one side of his face, so that it partially shielded his eyes from the glare of the headlamps. He shot coolly, methodi- cally, four shots in the space of four seconds. He did not expect to escape death this time. But the instinct of the fighting man made him want to take at least one enemy along with him on the Long Journey. And all four of his shots found their mark in the body of the machine gunner, smashing the man head over heels off the running board, to perform a backward somersault in the air, with the machine gun flying off at a tangent, unfired.

Klaw smiled grimly. He had got his man, anyway. Now, let the hurtling death strike him.

The imminence of death was no new thing to him. Kerrigan and Murdoch and Klaw had the reputation, in fact, of even *seeking* death. And it was whispered, in the dark and murky alleys of the underworld, that the Grim Reaper avoided them out of pure pique. They were called the Suicide Squad of the F.B.I., those three, and they had amply earned the name. No stale, routine assignments for them; only those jobs from which there was very little chance of ever coming back alive.

A year ago there had been five of them on the Suicide Squad. Six months ago, four. Yesterday, three—Kerrigan and Murdoch and Klaw. Today, if the report of Murdoch's death were true, there were only two. And if this murderous, hurtling newspaper truck made good its vicious attempt upon the life of Stephen Klaw, there would be only one.

But if Stephen Klaw could not see to shoot accurately against the blinding brilliance of those headlamps, there was another who could. Johnny Kerrigan was not in the line of the lights. Almost before the truck had got into motion, his heavy service revolver was in his hand. He moved without panic, without undue hurry—even though it seemed that only a second intervened before Klaw would be crushed to death. Kerrigan was used to gauging time in split-seconds. He knew that he would be vouchsafed one single shot—and if that shot missed, there'd be no use in a second, except for revenge.

CAREFULLY, JOHNNY Kerrigan rested the long barrel of the service revolver on the sill of the auto window, and bent his head to peer along the sight. He lined his gun on the right front tire of the speeding truck, held his breath, and pulled the trigger with a soft, gentle motion—and a prayer upon his lips.

The explosion blew a gust of powder back into his eyes, and the recoiling butt struck him in the forehead, so that for an instant he could not see the effect of his shot. The truck had been only twenty feet from Klaw when he fired. There was a chance....

He raised his head and leaned far out, in time to see the truck careening, as the right front tire exploded. The truck swayed sharply down on the flat, and the driver fought the wheel madly, desperately, in an effort to swing it back so that it would not miss Stephen Klaw. But the drag of the flat was too much for him. It carried the truck far over to the right, tearing the steering wheel from the driver's hands. The left front wheel missed Klaw by a matter of inches, and then the truck smashed into a hydrant. It tore the hydrant out by the roots, and a geyser of water spouted upward.

The vehicle didn't stop, but smashed ahead, to crash into the stone fence in front of the Municipal Park. It teetered for an instant on the two left wheels, then tipped, and crashed over on its side. Flames burst from the front part of it, and the driver tittered a scream which was heard even above the sudden tumult of noise which arose all around. Then the man's scream was smothered in the flame.

Kerrigan's face was a set mask of cold marble. He did not look in the direction of the burning truck, but over toward Stephen Klaw, who still stood in the middle of the street.

Klaw had put his gun back in his pocket. With that faint, little smile upon his lips, he framed two words: *"Thanks, Mope!"*

Kerrigan winked, and waved his hand. He put the service revolver away.

No one knew where the shots had come from. Indeed, it was questionable whether any of the passers-by even knew what had caused the wreck of the truck. Certainly, no one even noticed the slim, wiry figure of Stephen Klaw in the middle of the street, or connected him in any way with the flaming vehicle.

Slowly, he continued across toward the Morgue. He did not look back toward the wreck, nor did he feel much sympathy for the man who had died in it so horribly. That man had tried to commit murder in the most callous and heartless way. And he was only the first of many, Steve felt sure, who would make similar efforts, under orders from Duke Lafflin.

All of Stephen Klaw's faculties were concentrated upon his surroundings as he approached the front entrance of the gloomy old Morgue building. A crowd was gathering to watch the burning newspaper truck; people were running toward the scene from all directions. It would be a perfect set-up for a second murder attempt. And though Steve knew that Johnny Kerrigan would cover him until he got off the street, he didn't want Johnny to leave himself open to attack from behind. So he quickened his steps, and hurried into the dimly lit corridor of the home of the dead.

CHAPTER 4
WHEN CORPSES
COME UP FIGHTING

THERE WAS not a soul in evidence, inside. And this was strange, because the smash-up out on the street had made enough noise to wake anyone who was not dead. It was queer that some of the attendants had not come out to see what had happened.

The Medical Examiner's office was on the right of the corridor. The door was wide open, and Steve could see that no one was in there. Two other doors on the same side of the corridor were closed. On the left was an arched doorway with a small hall leading to a door upon which was lettered:

AUTOPSY ROOM

At the end of the corridor there was a staircase leading down into the basement. That, Steve decided, would probably be where the bodies were kept.

He hesitated a moment, wondering whether to have a look into the autopsy room, before going downstairs. As he stood there he could feel the slowly creeping cold which mounted from the refrigeration chamber below. He started toward the stairs in the rear.

A woman appeared, hurrying up those back stairs. Steve stopped with a jerk.

She was attired in a light summer dress, and the lines of her figure indicated that she was not wearing much of anything underneath it. Her hair was dark, and very carefully done. There was about her an air of expensive luxury.

She smiled very winningly, and came hurrying over to Steve.

"How do you do?" she said throatily. "Is there anything I can do for you?"

"Why, no," said Steve. "I guess not. I was looking for someone in charge—"

"I'm the one you want, then," she broke in. "I'm Wilma Rogers, the Medical Examiner's secretary. Can I help you?"

Steve Klaw raised his eyebrows. He looked her over once more. The dress she was wearing hadn't cost a cent less than fifty dollars. Her tooled-leather handbag was worth at least ten dollars, and her shoes and hat must have accounted for another twenty-five between them. The string of pearls around her throat was worth a small fortune, if he was any judge, and there was a diamond ring on one of her fingers that even an inexperienced eye would have estimated as being two carats or over.

"Lady," Steve told her, "the Medical Examiner must pay you a hell of a good salary."

She became frigid, and her chin tilted. "That's none of your business!"

"Sure," Klaw said pleasantly. "Let's skip it. Excuse me."

He made to pass around her and continue on toward the stairs, but she said hurriedly, "Oh, I—I didn't mean to hurt your feelings. Please—let me help you. Were you looking for anyone in particular?"

"Yes," said Steve. "A corpse. My name is Klaw. Stephen Klaw, of the F.B.I. I'm looking for the body of Dan Murdoch."

She sucked in her breath, sharply. "Oh—yes. Come—right this way!"

SHE LED him toward the autopsy room on the left, and he followed, with his hands in his jacket pockets.

"What did you say your name was?" he asked.

"Wilma Rogers," she told him.

"Glad to know you, Wilma," he said.

"Wasn't it dreadful," she hurried on, "about—about your friend, Mr. Murdoch? He—he was killed with a sawed-off shotgun. Most of his face was blown away." She shuddered very prettily, and opened the door of the autopsy room. "Right in here." She motioned for him to go first.

Steve grinned thinly, and took her arm. The sleeves of her thin dress did not reach her elbows, and her skin felt strangely flushed and hot, for such a cool place as the Morgue. Her face, too, was flushed. Her eyes avoided his.

Steve's fingers gripped her arm, and he propelled her into the autopsy room ahead of him. "Ladies first!" he said pleasantly.

"Don't you trust me?" she asked, in a hurt voice. "Do you think—I'd lead you into a trap?"

"Lady," Steve said, "you're too beautiful to trust…. And too anxious to please," he added.

She made no other objection to entering first, except to say, "I give you my word—there are only corpses in here."

Inside the autopsy room, Steve nodded, as he closed the door behind them. "My apologies, Wilma. I guess you were telling the truth."

There were four dissecting tables in the room, and a shrouded

106

corpse lay on each of them, with the sheets hanging low over the sides. Otherwise, the room was vacant. Cases of surgical scalpels, chemicals and dissecting instruments lined the walls. The place had the appearance of a quiet, well ordered laboratory, far removed from the threat of violence and crime.

Wilma Rogers cast a reproachful glance at Steve Klaw. "You G-men are terribly suspicious."

Steve had grown suddenly serious. "Which of these bodies is supposed to be Dan Murdoch?"

"I'll tell you in a minute, as soon as I look it up on the chart."

He followed her to the desk at the far end of the autopsy room, and she picked up a ruled sheet of paper. But instead of reading from the paper, she suddenly ducked around the other side of the desk, and ran, as swiftly as a deer, toward the door. She reached it, and snatched it open. Then she shouted, *"All right, give it to him!"* and sped out into the corridor, slamming the door behind her.

STEPHEN KLAW had started in pursuit, but when he heard her shout, he guessed what he was up against. He stopped dead in his tracks and swiveled around, both hands digging deep into his jacket pockets. A slow, tight grin of admiration tugged at his lips. Even now, he could give due credit for a good trick.

The four corpses on the dissecting tables had suddenly come to life. They threw off their shrouds and sat up, each one of them gripping a long-barreled automatic, which they swung toward Steve Klaw. Flame began to belch from those guns.

Steve didn't attempt to get the two automatics out of his jacket pockets. He merely thumbed off the safety catches, thrust the muzzles as far forward as he could against the lining of the pockets, and began to pull the triggers.

He was, therefore, about a second and a half ahead of the bogus corpses in opening fire. A bellowing blast of continuous thunder filled the room. Lead *zinged* past his ears and smashed into the wall behind him. He stood with legs wide apart, slim, yet firm as a rock against that four-fold barrage. His own automatics bucked in unison.

He got the two end men with the first two shots, sent them rolling off their dissecting tables—and this time they were really candidates for the coroner. Then his guns swung inward toward the two middle men.

Those two were shooting fast and furious, in sudden panic. From their faces it was evident that they had expected to cut him down before he could fire a shot. This business of trading bullets with a cool, collected fighting man was something different. If they could have got up and run away at that second, they probably would have done so. But there was nowhere to run, so they kept on shooting in desperation.

Suddenly the door was flung open, and the giant figure of Johnny Kerrigan appeared there, with a heavy revolver in each hand, and a fighting grin upon his face.

The deep, sonorous thunder of Johnny's two revolvers joined the sharp blasts of Stephen Klaw's automatics. Steve didn't look around. By the sound of those guns, he knew who was there. Together now, their weapons lanced blistering streamers of flame at the two remaining gunmen.

In another moment, the fight was over.

Four dead men lay on the floor, entangled in the shrouds in which they had posed as corpses. The echoing gunfire still reverberated through the building.

KERRIGAN SLAPPED Steve on the back. "So now you take to fighting dead men, eh, Shrimp?" he roared at his partner.

"Did you have to butt in, Mope?" Steve asked sourly. "I was handling it okay."

"That's the thanks I get!" Kerrigan grumbled. "I heard the shooting, and came on the run. And I get bawled out for butting in!"

"Did you see a girl out there in the hall?" Steve asked.

"Yes. She was high-tailing it out the back way. I let her go, and came in here. She's not bad on looks. Is she a friend of yours?"

"In a way," Steve grinned. "She provided this entertainment."

They stepped out into the hall, without bothering to search the four dead men. Johnny kept his guns in his hands, and Steve wiggled the muzzles of his automatics through the holes in his pockets.

Not a soul was in evidence. For some strange reason, no one had come to investigate the shooting.

"This is a hell of a town!" Kerrigan said. "Everybody must be deaf. First there's a shooting outside, and no one comes out of here to look. Then there's a shooting inside, and no one comes in from out there!"

"They must be cooking up a new one for us," Steve remarked. "What do you think they'll try next?"

Johnny shrugged. "It's all the same to me. Let them bring on anything they can think of—as long as they keep it interesting."

"Let's take this place apart," Steve said. "I want to see if they really have Dan's body in here."

The two of them started toward the staircase that led down to the refrigerator room. As they descended, they took turns reloading their guns, so that one of them was ready to shoot while the other loaded.

"What's the name of that dame that put you on the spot?" Johnny demanded.

"Wilma Rogers."

"She has nice ankles," Johnny said. "I'd like to know her better."

"So would I," Steve replied grimly. "But not for her ankles."

At the foot of the stairs there was a door with a sign which said:

NO ADMITTANCE
Except with Medical Examiner's Pass

"This is where they store the stiffs till they're buried," Johnny Kerrigan said. "If Dan is really dead, he'll be in here."

HE TRIED the door, and it opened under his touch. He kicked it wide open, and the two of them stepped through, side by side, guns in hand.

The temperature down here was frigid. A cold blast of air struck them as they entered. Three walls of the chamber were lined with niches, each furnished with a sliding slab which could be pulled out of the compartment for the purpose of viewing a corpse.

110

Three men stood beside one of the slabs, which had been drawn out of its niche. A shroud-covered body lay upon the slab.

Two in the group were in police uniform, and the third wore a frock coat and a pair of gold-rimmed pince-nez. They were bending over the body on the slab, but it was very evident that they were more interested in who was coming through the door than in the corpse. They stiffened as Kerrigan and Klaw appeared in the open doorway. A look of incredulous surprise appeared on their faces.

Johnny Kerrigan whispered to Steve, out of the side of his mouth: "These bozos heard the shooting, all right. They didn't expect to see us alive!"

"Must have been waiting for the girl to come down and report," Klaw replied.

The two of them sauntered across the room, with their guns dangling carelessly at their sides. The three men watched them, fascinated.

The one with the pince-nez glasses licked his lips. "Do—you have passes?" he asked. "No one is allowed in here without a pass."

"Sure," Johnny told him, with a grin. "Sure we have passes." He turned to Steve. "Haven't we, Mr. Klaw?"

"Why of course, Mr. Kerrigan. Let's show the gentleman our passes."

In unison, the two of them raised their guns and covered the others.

"These passes usually get us in anywhere, mister!" Kerrigan said. "Or would you like to argue about it?"

The man with the pince-nez took an involuntary step backward. But one of the uniformed men, who had police captain's bars on his collar, exclaimed, "See here, you two! You're laying yourselves open to arrest. Put those guns away. I'm Captain Draper, and this gentleman—" pointing to the one with the pince-nez—"is Doctor Fenwick, the Medical Examiner. Put those guns away!"

"Not yet, Captain," Stephen Klaw said grimly. "There are too many people in this town who use guns carelessly. Did you know, there was a little shooting upstairs?"

"Shooting?" Captain Draper frowned. "I—we—didn't hear a thing!"

"That's funny," Steve said tightly. "Damn funny!" Johnny said.

As they talked, they kept crossing the room, shoulder to shoulder. Captain Draper and the other policeman kept their hands conspicuously away from the holstered guns at their sides.

Medical Examiner Fenwick coughed nervously, and took off his pince-nez glasses and wiped them. "I'm sure there must be some mistake. You two gentlemen are F.B.I. agents, of course. I recognize the names. No one would try to shoot you in this town."

"No one," Steve broke in, "except your own secretary. A little girl named Wilma Rogers. She put me on the spot, all right. By the way, Doctor Fenwick, there's a little work for you upstairs. Those four phony corpses are real ones now."

Fenwick began to splutter denials. "I—I assure you, I don't know what you're talking about. I have no secretary named Wilma Rogers."

"That's fine," said Steve. "Let's forget about that for a minute. We're here to look at the body of Dan Murdoch. Where is he?"

"Right here," Fenwick said hastily, pointing to the covered body on the slab. "We—ah—were just about to—er—examine it—"

Steve stepped to one side of the slab, and Johnny to the other. They motioned the three men back, and stood in such a way that they could keep them covered. The faces of the two G-men were set and grim as Stephen Klaw reached down and slowly pulled the sheet off the body.

They both shuddered at sight of the mutilated face. The features had been entirely obliterated by the hail of slugs which had struck it.

They both looked swiftly away from the face, and down at the naked torso of the dead man. Their glance swung to the chest and arms. They had both fought side by side with Dan Murdoch, dozens of times. In those battles, none of them had gone unwounded. They knew where each other's wounds had been received, and where the scars of those injuries should be. They knew of at least five places where Murdoch had been hit, on different occasions. There should be a long scar high up on the right side of his chest, and two on his right arm above the elbow, and another across the hip.

But this body had none of those old wounds.

A thrill of fierce joy coursed through Stephen Klaw's veins. His face showed nothing of what he thought, but his eyes flickered as they rose to meet the eyes of Johnny Kerrigan. The look they exchanged was significant. Each knew that the other understood.

This was not the body of Dan Murdoch!

CHAPTER 5
MURDER GOES TO PRESS

CAPTAIN DRAPER'S hand was sneaking toward his holstered gun as Steve and Johnny swung to face the three men. Draper hastily snatched his hand away from the holster.

Kerrigan gave him a tight grin. "Any time, Captain Draper. Any time you like."

"What do you mean?" demanded the police captain, with an air of innocence.

"He means," Steve explained, "that he'd just like to see you pull that gun."

"I'll not be bullied like this!" Draper exclaimed indignantly. "Not by any four-flushing G-men. I demand that you put those guns away!"

Kerrigan didn't take his eyes off the captain, but he spoke to Steve. "He wants us to put our guns away, Mr. Klaw. Do you think we should oblige the gentleman?"

"Why certainly, Mr. Kerrigan. I think we should always try to oblige a gentleman, Mr. Kerrigan."

They both put their guns away, simultaneously—Johnny into his shoulder holsters, Steve into the jacket pockets with the holes in them.

"Now," Johnny suggested softly, "if you want to go for your guns—"

But none of the three men seemed willing to try that. Fenwick coughed again, and once more began to wipe his pince-nez.

"I hope you'll both remain for the inquest," he suggested mildly.

"Sure," said Steve. "We'll be around. We have some business to take care of in this town. And now, if you'll pardon us, we must be going."

He nodded to Kerrigan, and started across the room. Johnny waited, watching the three men, until Steve reached the door. Then, while Steve turned and watched them, Johnny crossed to join him.

"We'll be seeing you, gentlemen," said Steve.

They backed out of the door, and went up the stairs in leisurely fashion. Nobody came after them from down below.

Up in the corridor, their eyes met and they grinned. Johnny grabbed Steve's hand, and pumped it up and down violently.

"He's not dead, Shrimp! Dan's not dead!"

"So far, so good," Steve Klaw said, suddenly serious. "But where is that handsome Romeo? I'd like to kick his pants for the worry he's given us."

"He's probably holed up, somewhere in town, with that girl—Martha Gray. Probably can't get her out past Lafflin's men. Have you got the address she gave him in her letter?"

"Hell, no!" Steve said disgustedly. "She enclosed that in a second envelope inside the letter, and it was for his eyes alone.

You can't beat a woman for getting screwy ideas. They beat all hell."

"Screwy is right!" Kerrigan grumbled. "And our Handsome Dan is so touched by the trust she places in him, that he swears he'll respect her confidence!"

"So that leaves us with no place to go," Steve decided.

"We could take this damn town apart, street by street," Kerrigan said hopefully, "till we find them. It might take us quite a while. But it'd be fun."

Steve grinned. "You won't have time for that. Lafflin's little boys will be busy making it very hot for us from now on."

JUST THEN a Western Union messenger boy came in through the front entrance, and looked around helplessly. He was holding a telegram. He came down the corridor toward Johnny and Steve, and on the way he passed the open door of the autopsy room. He saw the four dead men on the floor, and he suddenly went yellow in the face. His knees began to wobble.

Johnny Kerrigan caught him under the arm. "Take it easy, sunny," he said. "Don't look in there any more. You'll be all right. I was sick as a dog too, the first time I saw a dead man."

"I—I'm looking for Mr. Kerrigan and Mr. Klaw," the boy stammered.

"That's us," Steve told him.

The boy handed over a telegram. Steve signed for it, gave the lad a quarter, and helped him to the door. Out front, there was still a crowd. A wrecking car was working on the smashed newspaper truck, and a crew was trying to extricate the burned driver.

Johnny joined Steve at the doorway, and Steve ripped open the envelope. The telegram said:

JOHN KERRIGAN & STEPHEN KLAW SILVERTON CITY MORGUE

COME QUICKLY AS I AM IN TERRIBLE DANGER. DO NOT DELAY OR IT MAY BE TOO LATE. MEN SURROUNDING WHOLE STREET. NOW THAT MURDOCH IS DEAD I DEPEND ON YOU TO GET ME OUT OF HERE. COME AT ONCE. AM STILL AT COOPER STREET ADDRESS.

MARTHA GRAY.

"Now that's damned funny," said Johnny Kerrigan. "How could Martha Gray have got the flash that we're at the Morgue? And how come she just says Cooper Street, instead of giving us the house number? She ought to know that she gave Dan that address confidentially."

"Also," Steve said thoughtfully, "she seems to think Dan is dead, and we know it's someone else. But Lafflin's men don't know that. They think they've got Murdoch's corpse down there."

"Therefore," Kerrigan finished, "we must assume that this telegram comes from Lafflin, and not from Martha Gray. Lafflin's little playmates know what street she's on, but not the house. They think we know. So they figure we'll be all excited by this telegram, and go straight to the Cooper Street house. They're counting on us to lead them to Martha Gray!"

A taxicab with the flag up swung around in front of the

Morgue, and the driver leaned out to open the door. "Cab, mister?" he called.

Steve was about to wave him away, for his own F.B.I. car was still parked across the Street. But Johnny stopped him.

"This guy seems pretty anxious to get us for passengers, Shrimp. Let's accommodate him."

Steve shrugged. "Why not? The way things are breaking tonight, I'd rather have both hands free to shoot, than tied up on a wheel!"

So they came out of the Morgue, and entered the cab.

"Drive over to Cooper Street," Kerrigan ordered.

THE DRIVER nodded, and swung the car around. As soon as he was in high, he glanced over his shoulder. "What number on Cooper Street, sir?" There was a slightly anxious edge in his voice, which both Steve and Johnny noticed.

"What numbers have you got?" Kerrigan asked.

The man scowled. "I don't get you, mister—"

Stephen Klaw suddenly got an inspiration. He poked Johnny in the side. Then he said out loud, "Why don't you stop kidding the poor man, Mr. Kerrigan? Tell him where you want to go."

Johnny looked at Steve blankly for a second, and then he stifled a grin as he got the idea.

"Sure, sure! I'm sorry, driver. It's my infernal sense of humor. We want to go to Sixty-one Cooper Street." He had chosen the first number that came into his head.

"Yes, *sir!*" said the driver, and turned his face forward again.

He drove rather slowly, which was extraordinary for a cab

driver, and it seemed that their route took them exclusively through mean and dark streets.

Johnny gave Steve a significant look.

There was an evening newspaper on the seat beside them, and Steve picked it up. It turned out to be the *Silverton Star-Gazette*, which was owned by Duke Lafflin. On page one, Steve spotted an item, and pointed it out silently to Johnny:

NOTED PUBLISHER TO VISIT SILVERTON

Nicholas Lafflin, the famous publisher, owner of a chain of newspapers of which the *Star-Gazette* is a member, is flying to Silverton for a personal visit. He will arrive tonight, for a short stay. Mr. Lafflin feels that he has not given as much attention so the *Star-Gazette* as it deserves, and he plans to inaugurate a series of innovations which will make this newspaper the most influential in the city. He has already mapped out a program to pep things up....

"I bet he'll pep things up!" Kerrigan whispered.

Stephen Klaw nodded grimly, his eyes sparkling. "And we'll do our best to make things lively for him!"

Their attention was taken from the newspaper by the sudden antics of the taxicab. It started to buck and rattle, and the motor backfired, then spluttered, and went dead.

"Aw, hell!" grunted the driver. "Can you imagine that? I'm outta gas!"

"You don't say!" said Johnny Kerrigan. "Does this happen to you often?"

119

"Naw. It's the first time in my life. I guess I forgot to fill up when I pulled out tonight."

"Will we have to walk home?" Steve asked.

"Naw. See, it's lucky we got stalled right here, in front of a garage."

He indicated a dark, squat building, with only a dim bulb above the double doors, which were closed. The sign over the doors said:

STAR-GAZETTE
SERVICE GARAGE

"I'll just go in there an' get a can of gas, an' then pull in an' fill up. It'll only take a minute."

"Sure, sure, go right ahead," Johnny told him, blandly.

The driver looked at him suspiciously for an instant, then turned and hurried into the garage.

As soon as he was inside, Steve said quickly, "Okay, Mope. Lets go!"

THEY JUMPED out of the cab and raced across the sidewalk to the garage entrance. They were not a moment too soon. Hardly had they reached the protection of the runway, when a bell somewhere inside sounded three sharp peals. Immediately, all hell broke loose about them.

A round, black object, about the size of a large grapefruit, came hurtling down from an upper window of the garage. Before it struck the cab, it was followed by a second and a third. The three missiles hit the roof of the cab a second or two apart, erupting with a series of terrific explosions which shook the

120

ground and shattered the taxicab into a twisted mass of unrecognizable wreckage.

Johnny Kerrigan and Stephen Klaw instinctively dropped to the ground, as bits of twisted metal flew all around them. The shattering reverberations almost split their ear drums.

Johnny uncovered his head and winked at Steve, as the thundering blast died away, and wreckage ceased to drop from the sky.

"Mills grenades!" he said. "Boy, those guys sure are trying hard!"

Steve grinned, and got to his feet. "Let's go in and congratulate them!" he said.

They took their guns out, and ran up the steep ramp. A few rumbling echoes of the explosion were still playing around the walls, but otherwise the big garage was silent.

At the top of the ramp they stopped a moment, and looked around. There were about two dozen *Star-Gazette* trucks parked up here—all similar to the one that had almost run Steve Klaw down in front of the morgue. Over toward the front were the windows from which the Mills grenades had been thrown down upon the taxicab. And two shadowy figures were hurrying along the wall toward the other end of the building.

At the far end there was a glassed-in office, from which light was streaming. Those two men hurrying toward the office were probably the grenade throwers.

Steve and Johnny slipped silently behind one of the parked trucks, and watched the pair disappear into that office. Then, when the way was clear, they ran on silent, rubber-soled shoes, across the cement garage floor. They stopped just outside the office door. A jumble of voices was coming from within, and one voice rose higher than the rest, apparently talking on the telephone. It was the voice of their taxicab driver.

"This is B-90 reporting!" he was saying in a high-pitched, excited tone. "Well, we got 'em, B-70! Wiped out the two of them—like flies. It worked like a charm. They gave me the address of that Martha Gray dame, an' then I drove around in front of the garage, like you said. I stalled, an' told them I was going in for gas, and they swallowed it. As soon as I got inside I rang the signal bell, an' the boys heaved the grenades. There ain't anything much left of that cab. It's a total loss—but so are those two damned G-men!"

B-90 paused for a moment, apparently listening, and then said, "Yeah. I got it, all right. Sixty-one Cooper Street. That's where they said they wanted to go, so that's where the Gray dame is holed up. Listen, B-70, do I get a bonus for this job? It finishes up the whole damned Suicide Squad!"

There was a little more talk, and then B-90 hung up.

They heard him discussing the job with the other two, and then one of them said, "Let's clear outta here. The cops have been tipped off to come in slow motion, but we might as well not be around. Put that typewriter away, Whitey. We won't need it no more—"

STEPHEN KLAW, outside the door, looked at Johnny Kerrigan. "That's our cue, Mope!"

Johnny grinned, and put his hand on the knob. He turned,

and pushed hard. The door swung wide open. The two G-men came through like a whirlwind.

The three men inside uttered startled yelps. B-90, their taxi driver, was spinning the cylinder of a revolver, while another of the trio was patting a sub-machine gun which he was about to place in a case on the desk. This one, whom they had heard addressed as Whitey, had a long, pinched face, and murderous little eyes. His hair was a dull black, but there was a long streak of white down the middle. The third man was behind Whitey, occupied in packing half a dozen Mills grenades into a valise.

Kerrigan and Klaw stopped just inside the doorway with their guns drawn, watching with amusement the effect of their abrupt appearance.

B-90 jumped two feet in the air, and swung his revolver up, pulling the trigger instinctively. Whitey leaped backward, and raised the sub-machine gun to his shoulder. The third man squealed and dropped the Mills grenade he was holding. It struck the floor, but luckily the pin had not been drawn, so it landed harmlessly, without exploding.

Whitey's finger was on the machine gun trip when Steve Klaw shot him through the head. Kerrigan turned his fire on B-90, and let him have a slug in the heart. B-90's first shot had gone into the floor because he had pulled the trigger too fast, and he never had a chance to fire another.

The third man pushed his hands high up in the air and yelled, *"Don't shoot! I quit!"*

Stephen Klaw grinned thinly. "I'll say you're quitting—for a long time!"

He crossed over the two dead bodies, and snapped a pair of bracelets on the man's wrists, running the chain around the radiator pipe in the corner. Johnny picked up the Mills grenade and put it in the valise with the others.

"We may need these tonight," he said.

"What's your name?" Steve demanded of the prisoner.

"Snell," whined the man. "Leo Snell."

"Who was B-90 talking to on the phone just now?"

"So help me, mister. I don't know. It was the one that gives us orders—B-70. It's a dame, but I don't know her name."

"Do you work regularly for the *Star-Gazette?*"

"Yes. I'm one of the lottery collectors. All the boys in town who collect for the lottery have to be trigger men—in case of trouble."

"And you don't know who you work for?"

"Gosh, mister, everyone in town knows that Duke Lafflin is behind the lottery. But no one can prove it. All I could tell you is that I collect the lottery dough, and turn it over to Tony Bragg. That's this guy here, that you shot—B-90. He turns it over to B-70. If he was alive, he might be able to tell you who she is."

"I think I know!" Steve Klaw murmured.

He turned to Johnny Kerrigan. "So now it would appear that Wilma Rogers, if she's B-70, is under the impression that we are good and dead. She'll so report to Lafflin, when he arrives here."

"You know," Johnny said thoughtfully, "that makes an interesting situation. They've got Dan down for dead, and now they have *us* marked off the slate. Which makes us practically ghosts. As ghosts, we can operate with a great deal of freedom. Ghosts can go through walls and things, and get into places that living men can't reach. We might even arrange a seance—with revolver obbligato!"

"My thought, exactly!" Steve said, with a grin. "Let's go!"

Kerrigan picked up the valise full of Mills grenades, and Steve took the sub-machine gun.

"Now be a nice boy," Kerrigan told Leo Snell, "and stick close to that radiator pipe. Don't go out tonight. There'll be lots of fireworks, and guys getting shot up. You'll be much better off staying right here—till we come back for you!"

They went out, and closed the office door behind them. Then they examined the newspaper trucks parked on the floor, and selected one that seemed to be in good condition and had a tankful of gas. They deposited the Mills grenades and the sub-machine gun in the back, and then Johnny got behind the wheel.

"Here go a couple of ghosts!" Johnny grinned.

Kerrigan drove the truck skillfully down the ramp, out past the wrecked taxicab, and headed east toward Cooper Street.

CHAPTER 6
HAVEN IN HELL

SIXTY-ONE COOPER was only a block from Fourteen, where Murdoch was holed up with Martha Gray, but Kerrigan and Klaw didn't know it. They drove the truck past Sixty-one, and at sight of what had taken place there, they began to have additional respect for the ruthless efficiency of Duke Lafflin's organization. It was only twenty minutes or so since B-90 had transmitted the address over the phone to B-70, who was presumably Wilma Rogers. Yet, in that short space of time, they had struck.

The street was full of fire apparatus. Thick smoke was emanating from the basement, as well as from one of the third floor windows. Lafflin's men had evidently hurried here, and started fires in the building. They had deliberately committed arson to flush Martha Gray from her hiding place.

Kerrigan drove on, grim-faced. "What will they do when they discover Martha Gray isn't in there?" he murmured.

Steve shrugged. "They'll probably keep their army of gunmen on watch in Cooper Street. The whole street is only four blocks long."

Near the corner, Kerrigan suddenly uttered an exclamation, and nudged Steve Klaw. He nodded to a blue roadster, parked facing the fire. Sitting at the roadster's wheel was beautiful Wilma Rogers.

"Well!" Steve said. "Here's your chance to become better acquainted."

Johnny made a complete U turn at the corner, came back and pulled up directly behind the roadster. The blue car's top was up. Wilma Rogers couldn't see who was in the truck behind her.

Many Lafflin gunmen, who had been watching the block, had gone over to assist those at the fire. No one paid any attention to the truck. Johnny remained at the wheel, while Steve climbed out and got on the roof. There he could see up and down the street.

He had barely reached his perch, when something small and

hard *plopped* down on the roof at his feet, and then bounced off into the gutter. The thing was a small frying pan.

He frowned, and looked up in the direction it had come from.

"For the love of mud!" he yelled. *"Hey, Johnny!"*

IN A moment, Johnny Kerrigan was at his side, and the two of them stared up at the fourth floor window of Number Fourteen, two doors down. The familiar mug of Dan Murdoch, smeared with a wide grin, was peering down at them. Over his shoulder, they saw the blurred figure of a girl. Murdoch waved, motioned them to come up, then disappeared.

But in that short space of time, the damage was done. A man on the roof of a private house across the street began to shout and gesticulate. He had a pair of binoculars, and it was evident that he had been posted there to watch for just such a thing. No doubt he had spotted Martha Gray with his high-powered glasses.

Kerrigan and Klaw sprang down from the roof of their truck. Already, four or five gunmen were flocking into Fourteen. Other men were on that roof.

"Let's go, Johnny!" Steve said. "This is the pay-off!"

They set out at a dead run for Number Fourteen, but arrived a second too late. The gunmen who had thronged into the building, had locked the door from the inside. There was no time to stop and break it down, for other hoodlums were racing from the burning building in the next block, and already shots were spattering around them.

"Let's flank them!" Steve shouted, and raced for the doorway of Number Sixteen, next door. He reached it first. Johnny

127

stopped twice to cover them, turning and emptying one gun at a time at the approaching gangsters. That slowed them up till he, too, reached the doorway. Then Steve turned and gave them a volley.

The wide, suburban road was echoing and re-echoing to the thunder of gunfire. A sub-machine gun, somewhere in the street, opened up on them with its staccato *rat-a-tat*, but they were already inside the hallway of Number Sixteen, had closed and locked the door.

They took the steps two at time, racing for the roof. Doors opened and closed as they passed. No householder was going to stick his neck out.

At the top, Johnny climbed the skylight ladder first. He thrust the trapdoor open with a mighty lunge of his shoulder. He leaped up on the roof. Steve was beside him.

Machine gun fire blazed at them from the roof of Number Fourteen. It was a little high, the hail of slugs crumbling the chimney behind them.

Both Johnny and Steve threw down on the gunner, fired at the same time. The man had been crouched behind the parapet of Fourteen's adjoining roof, with only his eyes showing. Four slugs hit him, and there was nothing left of his head.

Kerrigan and Klaw took the parapet in a flying broad jump, and raced for the skylight of Fourteen. It was open, but some-one down in the hall started sending a hail of machine gun slugs up through the opening. Two gunners evidently commanded the skylight, for the vicious rain of lead never ceased. Merely to look over that skylight meant death, let alone trying to climb through it. Apparently, the gunners were determined to keep help from coming down, till they could finish Murdoch in the apartment below.

Johnny Kerrigan, watching the bullets fly, shook his head. "I should have brought one of those Mills grenades," he said.

STEVE MOTIONED toward the front of the house, and ran in that direction. He looked over the parapet, saw they were just above the fire ladder. Three gunmen were on the ladder in front of Dan Murdoch's window. Two had sub-machine guns, the third a revolver. Other thugs were coming up the ladder. The gangsters were pounding the apartment interior with machine gun fire. It was apparent that Murdoch and the girl had been driven either into another room, or into a corner not exposed to the deadly slugs.

"I'm going down, Johnny!" Steve yelled. "Cover me!"

He scrambled over the parapet and fairly leaped down the ladder, his guns thundering. Above him, Johnny Kerrigan's two heavy revolvers roared, as he fired, skillfully and accurately, past Steve's hurtling form.

A thug screamed, threw up his hands, and went toppling over the side of the fire platform. Another clutched his stomach and doubled over. But others had already reached the landing from below, and they turned their guns up at Stephen Klaw.

Steve emptied his automatics into them, then hit the platform like an avalanche. He grappled with one gunman on the floor of the fire escape, as another, with a sub-machine gun, and a third, with a blasting automatic, clambered up on the landing.

Lead fanned Steve's cheek as he clinched with the gunman on

the floor. His opponent was powerful, but Stephen Klaw's slim, wiry body possessed terrible strength. Steve got a grip around the other's neck with his right arm, pounded with his left fist. The thug tried a kick in the groin, but Steve knew all about that.

The other two hoods had turned their weapons on the roof, where Johnny Kerrigan, guns empty, had started clambering down the ladder. The torpedo with the Tommy gun swung it up, and grinned wickedly. His lips curled in a snarl.

"Take it, Sucker—"

That was all he said, because suddenly an avalanche erupted onto the fire escape from the window. Dan Murdoch, relieved of the withering machine gun fire which had kept him out of line with the window, came into action.

He reached out, seized the gunner's leg, and yanked. The man came down, grappling with Dan, while the third hood bent over them, trying to get a shot at Murdoch's back. Then, something like a comet came hurtling down the ladder from the roof.

Kerrigan hit the man with all of his hundred and ninety pounds, smashing him against the wall of the house. Then he picked up the thug who was grappling with Steve, lifted him by the collar, and drove a big fist into his face. The man collapsed, and Johnny let him slide to the floor. Dan Murdoch had his man under control—but, for good measure, he smacked the gunmen's head once against the wall.

They were victorious—temporarily.

Murdoch grinned. "Hiya, Shrimp? Hiya, Johnny?" he said.

They grinned back. Johnny patted him on the shoulder.

Steve looked in through the window, and saw the scared face

of Martha Gray peering out at them. He smiled, and whispered to Murdoch, "How's the little love nest getting along?"

Murdoch scowled. "Love nest, my eye. Martha Gray is a sweet little kid. But she's scared as hell. I couldn't get her to take a chance on my shooting our way out of here, and she wouldn't even let me go out alone and try to contact you mugs. So all I could do was sit here and hope someone would show up."

"And then you said hello with a frying pan!"

They were talking, out there, with as much unconcern as if the street and the roofs hadn't been filled with men bent on killing them.

It was Johnny who spied the first of them peering over the roof, the stock of a Tommy gun alongside his face.

Johnny snapped a revolver up, but it was empty, and only clicked. Steve did the same, but both his automatics were empty. The gunman grinned down at them, aimed carefully, with his hand on the trip.

MURDOCH HADN'T done much shooting from inside the apartment, and he still had cartridges. He snapped a shot upward, and the gunner's face disintegrated under the impact of the heavy .45 slug.

"Nice work, Dan," Johnny said.

"I think we better go inside," Steve said. "The air is not as good inside, but it's quieter."

They climbed in, just as men in the street opened fire with high-powered rifles. Powerful .30-30 slugs ripped through the window, smashed the ceiling and the upper part of the walls. At the same time, gunmen in the hall loosed a barrage into the door. Lead flew through the apartment, piercing the lightly plastered walls from the hall into the living room, where they were gathered.

Martha Gray cowered against Dan Murdoch, shivering. Murdoch winked at the boys, and put an arm around her shoulder.

"Take it easy, Martha," he told her. "We'll get you out of here with a whole skin—or none of us will get out. That's a promise!"

They didn't bother watching the window, for as long as those high-powered rifles continued to fire, no one could come down from the roof.

"I'll be damned!" Kerrigan rasped. "Lafflin must own this whole town. Imagine a battle like this going on, and the cops don't even show up!"

Martha Gray raised her head from Murdoch's shoulder. "You—you better hope the cops *don't* come. That Captain Draper commands them, and he takes orders from Lafflin. He—he'd tell his men that you were fugitives from justice or something, and they'd attack with tear gas!"

"Sounds very unpromising," Stephen Klaw said. "I think we better be going. There's too much noise around here to suit me!"

"Okay by me," Murdoch clipped.

"By me, too," Kerrigan echoed, shouting to make himself heard above the racket of the gunfire.

"What'll it be?" Murdoch asked. "Window or door?"

"I think the door is best," Steve decided. "Let's go—"

But Martha Gray clutched at Dan's sleeve. "Wait! You—you're going to leave me here?"

"Not a chance, baby," Murdoch told her. "We'll take you right with us."

"But—but all the shooting—"

Dan pressed her arm. "It's the only thing to do, Martha. If you stay here, they'll get you eventually. Always remember what Napoleon said: *'The best defense is to step right up and smack your opponent in the schnozzle!'* "

"Nap—Napoleon w-wouldn't have used s-such language!" she sobbed.

"He would," Dan assured her, "if he were alive right now."

THE THREE loaded their guns swiftly. Then Kerrigan and Klaw stepped toward the hall door. Murdoch brought up the rear, keeping Martha Gray behind him.

Steve and Johnny stopped for a minute, peering around the corner into the hall. The hail of slugs sweeping in through the door was about waist high, apparently coming from two alternating machine guns. After each drum was exhausted, there was a pause of a few seconds. It took less time to empty a drum that to load one. They waited, timing the switch of guns. The looked-for pause came. Steve and Johnny, both crouched low, raced down the short hall to the door.

Johnny raised both guns. Steve twisted the lock and yanked the door open. As soon as it opened, Johnny began triggering his two heavy revolvers. In a split-second he was joined by Stephen Klaw. They sent a sudden hail of sweeping lead out at the two stunned machine gunners, who had thought they were in absolute security, never dreaming that the Suicide Squad would make a break.

That blast from the four guns in the hands of the two G-men cut the gunners down in a trice. Four others were out there on the landing, apparently waiting for a chance to rush the apartment when the door caved in. A couple of gunmen were up on the roof. They came running to the skylight when they heard the deep, sonorous roar of the revolvers taking the place of the sharp staccato drumfire.

Kerrigan concentrated on the men on the landing, while Klaw turned his twin automatics up toward those near the skylight. Dan Murdoch came up behind them and stuck his guns out, to augment the deadly threnody of doom which his partners' weapons were singing.

The four men on the landing went down like wheat under a scythe. Klaw's guns brought one of the thugs toppling down through the skylight to crash on the landing. The other hung limply over the edge, blood dripping down from his neck.

Kerrigan, Murdoch and Klaw stopped shooting. With flying fingers they reloaded their weapons. Then, Steve and Johnny went among the dead, picked up two sub-machine guns, and fitted drums of cartridges into them.

"Contact established with the enemy," piped Johnny Kerrigan. "Advance elements of the enemy forces have been met and annihilated. Large quantities of arms and ammunition have been captured. Send that out on the wires, Corporal Klaw, and inform the War Department that we expect to contact the main body of the enemy within X minutes. Have you got that, Corporal Klaw?"

"I have it, Colonel Kerrigan. The general sends his compliments, and wants to know what you'll have for dinner."

"If I eat with the angels tonight, I want ambrosia. If I eat on earth, make it a juicy medium-rare steak, with French fried potatoes and onions."

"Phooey!" said Dan Murdoch. "Me, I want a shrimp cocktail, and then some tender broiled lobster."

"Scrambled eggs and toast for me," Klaw said. "You shouldn't eat heavy, unless you do heavy exercise. You guys want to get fat, and be retired on a pension?"

Martha Gray looked from one to the other of them with wide eyes. They were doing it for her benefit, to keep her spirits up, but it did even more than that. She suddenly started to smile. "I—I think it would be wonderful—just to *die* with you three!" she gulped.

"Attagirl!" approved Murdoch, clapping her on the back. "Here's a gun. Know how to use it?"

"Certainly. You point it at someone, and then you pull the trigger."

"You learn fast, Martha," Dan told her. "We may yet make a man out of you!"

"God forbid!" she laughed.

The four of them went clattering down the stairs, with guns ready for whatever might be awaiting them in the street.

CHAPTER 7
" 'TILL DEATH DO US PART"

FOR A long time to come they will talk about the "Battle of Cooper Street." The story of that fight, the story of four men and a girl against the forces of Duke Lafflin's immense crime empire, seized the popular imagination with irresistible appeal.

They came storming out the front door of Number Fourteen with guns flaming like the artillery of hell.

It was Dan Murdoch who yanked the street door open, while Kerrigan and Klaw knelt just inside, with the sub-machine guns at their shoulders.

Outside, Lafflin's snipers were still peppering the window with high-powered rifles, not knowing that the apartment up there was deserted. The first intimation they had of the counter-attack was Murdoch's shrill whistle, which cut through the continuous, spiteful barking of the rifles like the shrieking of an airplane's wing-struts in a high wind.

The riflemen looked over to the doorway, and saw the two grim G-men, sub-machine guns ready.

Some hoods screamed, threw down their rifles, and ran. Others, out of reflex impulse, swung their rifles to the new point of danger. It was only then, when the rifles were actually pointing at them, that Steve shouted, *"Give it to 'em, Johnny!"*

They pulled their trips together, sent a withering blast of lead across the street. Those riflemen were cut down like so much chaff. And then, the three G-men came marching out of the doorway, shoulder to shoulder, guns blasting, Martha Gray behind them, covering the rear. There were still half a dozen machine gunners in the street, and these turned their weapons on the advancing trio. But Kerrigan and Klaw, on either side of Murdoch, kept their drumfire rolling, sweeping burst after burst down the length of the street.

The hoods could take so much, and no more. After three or four of them dropped, the others threw away their weapons and ducked for safety into any doorway that offered refuge. They didn't stop going, either, but disappeared out the back way and were never heard from again.

In a matter of minutes, the street was cleared of opposition.

Kerrigan and Klaw still had half a drum apiece in their rapid-firers, and Murdoch hadn't even used all of the cartridges in his revolvers, when they ceased firing.

Murdoch swung around and patted Martha Gray's arm.

"Good girl—"

He was interrupted by a hoarse shout from Johnny Kerrigan.

Johnny was pointing at the blue roadster they had seen before, with Wilma Rogers at the wheel. It was racing toward them now, Wilma still driving. There was someone in the seat beside her. The man was leaning far out, and he had a machine gun resting on the sill. All three of them recognized that man.

They had seen his picture a hundred times in the papers.

It was Duke Lafflin himself!

LAFFLIN HAD come to Silverton, personally to direct the killing of Martha Gray and the annihilation of the Suicide Squad. He had sat here, with Wilma Rogers, and had watched that headstrong trio wipe out his armed gunmen, and bring Martha Gray out to safety—Martha Gray who could talk and incriminate him!

This must have been too much for Lafflin to bear. His face, now screwed up into a mask of terrible venom as he sighted along the gun, was a reproduction of hatred that surpassed anything human. He was witnessing the break-up of his vicious empire of crime, and he was going to make one more last try—personally—to destroy the Suicide Squad and the girl who could ruin him.

Wilma Rogers sent the blue roadster spinning down the street toward the trio, crushing the bodies of dead and wounded. Nothing mattered now! The Suicide Squad must be wiped out!

Kerrigan and Klaw once more raised their guns. Murdoch thrust Martha Gray behind him, and threw down with both revolvers on the hurtling roadster.

Lafflin began to shoot at the same time. But he was shooting from a racing car, and they were standing still. He was in the grip of deep and hateful emotion, and they were still the same cool and collected fighting men they had always been.

The result could not be in doubt. They only regretted that it was impossible to avoid hitting Wilma Rogers.

Both of them were dead before the blue roadster, out of control, mounted the sidewalk and crashed into a brownstone house across the street. It bent like a tin can, and burst into flame.

Kerrigan and Murdoch and Klaw stood solemnly with Martha Gray, and watched the blazing funeral pyre of Wilma Rogers and Duke Lafflin—Duke Lafflin, the man who had likened himself to Nero, to Bonaparte, to Hitler and Stalin. Like all men who seek inordinately after power to which they have no right, he had come to a bitter and terrible end.

It was long after the fire engines from down the street had succeeded in putting out the fire in the wrecked machine, that Kerrigan and Murdoch and Klaw got into a cab with Martha Gray.

All were sober and quiet.

"God help us," Dan Murdoch said, "we've killed a lot of men tonight!"

Steve Klaw nodded. "And as long as we stay in the Service, we'll have to kill more—and more. It's—our job!"

Martha Gray clutched at Dan Murdoch's sleeve. "Dan!" she whispered. "Why—don't you give it up! Leave this terrible job! You—we—could be so happy—"

Dan stroked her shoulder. His eyes softened. Then he looked up and saw Kerrigan and Klaw watching him quizzically, with an amused glint in their eyes.

He flushed. Then he took the girl's hand off his sleeve.

"Martha," he said firmly, "I'm practically married to these two roughnecks. I'm tied to them—till death do us part!

He looked up and met the eyes of Kerrigan and Klaw once more, and the lips of the three of them formed the words: *"Till death do us part!"*

THE SUICIDE SQUAD
AND THE MURDER BUND

CHAPTER 1
A WOMAN DIES

A KEEN October wind was cutting across the Drive from the Hudson when Stephen Klaw came out of the side street. He stopped in the lee of the corner apartment building, and lit a cigarette. He did not at once put out the match, but held it cupped in front of his face so that his clean-cut though rugged features were illuminated.

Almost at once, a woman came darting from the shadows of the park across the street. She was dressed in a black raincoat, and wore no hat. Her dark hair streamed out behind her as she ran, in zig-zag fashion, as if wounded. And the great spreading stain of crimson upon the black background of the raincoat, just underneath the heart, testified to the wound.

Under her right arm she was clutching a small black leather brief-case, which seemed to be more precious to her than the life blood which was pouring from her body.

Before she had taken half a dozen steps across the wide expanse of Riverside Drive toward Stephen Klaw, a man's voice rose in a triumphant shout, hoarse and vindictive: *"There she is!"*

The man came tearing out from the park, a little farther down the block. At the same time, two other men broke from cover,

at other points along the Drive. They had evidently been combing the park for her. All three of them converged upon her. They had peculiar weapons—the stocks resembled those of Thompson sub-machine guns, but the barrels were sawed-off so that they were only about six inches long.

Stephen Klaw's lips pursed tightly when he saw those guns in the hands of the three men. He spat the cigarette from his lips, and thrust his hands down into his jacket pockets. They emerged almost at once, each gripping an automatic.

The first of those three pursuing men dropped to one knee, and aimed his sawed-off machine-gun, while the other two raised their weapons to their shoulders to fire as they ran. All three muzzles were concentrated upon the back of the staggering woman. Either they had not seen the slim, almost boyish figure of Stephen Klaw, or else they did not connect him with their quarry.

Klaw's eyes were cold and hard as he fired both automatics from the hip. The men on the extreme right and left of the running woman fell as those two automatics began their spiteful, deadly barking. They never even fired their weapons.

But the third, directly behind the woman, was shielded from Klaw by her staggering body.

The fellow saw his advantage at once, and dropped flat on the ground, raising his sawed-off machine-gun and pulling the trip at the same time. A burst of scattering lead belched from the mouth of the vicious weapon, spreading over a radius of twenty feet, something like the buckshot from a small-gauge shotgun.

Stephen Klaw had anticipated this tactic. There was only one thing he *could* do, and he did it without reflection or hesitation. Almost before his two automatics had ceased thundering, he launched himself in a flying tackle, straight at the running woman. He reached her a split instant before the sawed-off machine-gun belched forth its lead.

KLAW'S SHOULDER struck the woman's legs and she

fell over him, landing so that his body was between her and the machine-gunner. The spray of lead whistled through the air, just above their heads. The man had fired high, evidently hoping to riddle the woman's body from the waist up. Only a few of the pellets arced low enough to strike Klaw, and he barely felt them as he fired his right-hand automatic from his prone position on the ground. His slug took the machine-gunner square in the forehead, and the man just relaxed and lay still.

Stephen sprang to one knee and knelt beside the dark-haired woman. She was trying feebly to stir. A moan escaped from her lips. The wound in her breast was bleeding profusely, and though she had escaped the leaden hail from the machine-gun, Klaw could see at a glance that she had not long to live. She raised a haggard face to his.

"Did—did they get you—too?"

He put a hand on her shoulder. "No. Only a few little nicks. I'll be able to pluck them out, easily."

"Thank… God… you're safe. I knew… they were looking… for me in the park. But I had to… keep the appointment with you. They got me with a lucky shot when I escaped with the brief-case. I wouldn't have lasted much longer…."

"I got the three of them," Stephen Klaw said grimly. "If that's any consolation. Now, I'm going to call an ambulance—"

"No, no. I'm… through—done for. Take the brief-case. It contains the list… I promised to get for you. All the names of the Executive Council… of… Skull and Swastika Corps!"

Klaw took the black leather case. He did not open it. He bent low over the dying woman.

145

"You've done a great service for your country, Mary Watson—"

"No, no. It's only… small part. You… must do the… rest. I got all names except the… leader's. His name was… Franz Trebizond… in Germany. I don't know… what name he uses in this country. That is for you… to find…."

The blood was pumping out of her body at an appalling rate. She should have been dead, but she was clinging to life by a terrible effort of naked will power.

"Look out for… Franz Trebizond. He is clever, ruthless—a blond beast without mercy or heart. And watch for the woman, Lisa Monterey. She is… bad as he…."

Mary Watson gasped, and a spasm went through her body. But she held on to life for another moment, with a grim purposeful effort.

"You must promise me… one thing more…."

"Anything you ask," Steve said.

"Promise to look after my daughter, Sue. They—the Skull and Swastika Corps—will try to hurt her because of what I did to them." She shuddered, and pressed a hand against her breast as if to stem the tide of spilling blood for one instant more. "I—I can't bear to think of Sue in the hands of those monsters. They… know dreadful tortures… they know where to find every living nerve in a girl's body. They would keep her in agony for days and days—"

"No, they won't," Stephen Klaw said grimly. He took a deep breath. "I give you my word, Mary Watson," he said solemnly, "and I give you the word of Kerrigan and Murdoch too. The three of us will see to it that nothing happens to Sue Watson—while we're alive!"

A look of ineffable happiness came into the swiftly-dimming eyes of Mary Watson, erasing the mask of pain from her features. Her body, relaxed, giving way at last to the sweet, blank nothingness of death.

She lay still....

CHAPTER 2
CODE FOR KILLERS

STEPHEN KLAW put a finger upon the artery in her throat. There was no pulse, no life. Slowly, he picked up the brief-case, and rose to his feet. As he looked down upon the still body of Mary Watson, there was a tight gray bleakness in his face, which had not been there before.

Sounds arose about him, in the quiet night air. Fifty heads were poked out of apartment house windows, and voices called out in fright and in execration.

"There's the murderer.... He killed the woman.... It's the Skull and Swastika again—I recognize those machine-guns! *Call the police! Catch him! Catch the murderer!*"

Men were running out of the corner house, others were coming from up and down the street. From a ground floor window a man's voice came clearly, high-pitched and keen: *"Operator! Operator! Get police headquarters! It's a killing! The Skull and Swastika...."*

Stephen Klaw paid no attention to the shouts, to the people

who stared out of the window, or to those who were in the street. His lips moved faintly as he stood over the body of the dark-haired woman.

"I don't like leaving you here, Mary Watson, dead in the gutter. But you were a brave woman. You would understand."

Instinctively, his right hand, holding the still-hot automatic, rose to his forehead in mute salute. Then, with the brief-case under his left arm, and an automatic in each hand, he turned and strode away down the same side street from which he had come. He looked neither to the right nor to the left, walking as if all those shouting, gesticulating, threatening people did not even exist.

They kept their distance, too, for the sight of those dead bodies on the ground, and of the automatics in his hands, was enough to deter the boldest of them from attempting to stop him.

But they yelled and they screamed, and they blasphemed against him.

"Damned Nazi," he heard. And, *"He's a Skull and Swastika gunman. Get the yellow rat!"*

A grim smile of irony tugged at Stephen Klaw's lips, at the thought that he should be reviled as a member of the vicious Fifth Column organization which he was fighting to the death. But he couldn't stop and explain to these people that he was an agent of the F.B.I., acting *sub rosa*, and without official commission. That was a secret between himself and his Chief. Yet he liked the sound of those epithets which were flung at him, because it reflected the temper of the American people. Americans were not ones to accept the activities of such an organization, as people of other countries had done, to their own cost.

These were the men and the descendants of men who had made America great and strong. These were men who had fought in the last world war, and who wanted only peace for this generation of their sons. Yet they were ready and willing to hurl themselves unarmed, against an armed enemy who was boring from within to destroy their cherished institutions and their cherished liberty.

Klaw smiled, like a fond elder brother. He fired twice into the air, then turned and took to his heels. It was the first time in recorded history that Stephen Klaw had run from danger!

As police sirens shrilled in the distance, the pursuing crowd raised a great shout. They had their man trapped. Steve knew well enough, that once he were caught now, even those bluecoats in the police car would not be able to keep him from being battered to a pulp by the fierce revengeful fists of his pursuers. There had been too many hideous tortures and wanton killings in recent weeks on the part of the Skull and Swastika Corps, and the citizens were out for blood. He must escape—quickly. He must reach the place where he had left his car in the next side street.

Steve swung into an open lot, as he had previously planned. But before he was halfway across the lot, a bullet whined past his head, followed by another and another. The stentorian voice of one of the bluecoats in the police car bellowed after him, *"Stop! Or we'll shoot to kill!"*

STEPHEN KLAW kept on running. He bent low from the

waist, holding tight to the brief-case which Mary Watson had bequeathed to him. He heard the police officer curse behind him, and shout, "All right, you asked for it!"

Only then did Klaw throw himself forward at full length on the ground. The policeman's gun bellowed, and a bullet screamed through the air, followed by another and another in quick succession.

"He's down!" some one shouted. "You got him—"

"Naw!" yelled the cop. "He dropped before I fired—"

Klaw jumped up, and started to run once more. He was almost into the mouth of the alley now, with only a low fence intervening. He hurdled the fence on the run, just as the cop fired again. He almost felt the tug of that bullet against his coat as he went over the fence into the alley beyond.

Now he raced through the alley out into the street beyond, with the hue and cry rising behind him to a shrilling crescendo of fury. His margin of safety was small, but it was enough for him. He was in his car, and had it started before the first of the pursuing throng came out into the street after him.

Without putting on his lights, he sent the car roaring away, and turned the far corner on two wheels. A couple of desultory shots followed him, but they were ineffective. In a moment he was away from all pursuit.

He switched on his radio, and drove south on Broadway, listening to the short-wave alarms which were being broadcast for him. The police were still under the impression that he was an operative of the Skull and Swastika Corps, and they were instituting a thorough manhunt. But they didn't have the license of his car, nor the make, for it had been too dark back there on that side street. Neither did they have a good description of him.

Grimly he opened the brief-case as he drove. He was surprised to find that it contained only a single sheet of paper, with a series of heiroglyphics written in vertical columns, as the Chinese write.

There were nine of these vertical lines, each containing from fifteen to thirty characters. Glancing at it swiftly as he drove, Klaw was unable to decide whether the characters were Chinese, or some less known alphabet of Indo-China or Malaysia. But there was no time to waste in deciphering this puzzle now. Mary Watson had said that this paper contained the names of the Executive Council of the Skull and Swastika, *but not the present identity of Franz Trebizond,* which Klaw wanted more than anything else. But first, there was one other thing which he must make sure of—a thing for which he had pledged his word, and the word of his two partners, Kerrigan and Murdoch.

When he reached the Eighties, he turned off and drove half way down the block until he reached a small apartment house set between a garage and a public playground. The playground was dark and deserted now, but the garage was busy.

Klaw did not stop in front of the apartment house. He merely glanced at it as he drove past, and swung his car into the garage. A sign on the outside said, PARKING—50 cents.

Ile left his car here, paid the fee and got a parking ticket. Then he walked out, stood at the curb for a moment while he lit a cigarette. He glanced up at the façade of the apartment house next door, fixing his glance for an instant on the first-floor window nearest the garage. There was a light in that window. He waited at the curb, smoking the cigarette slowly. A minute passed. Then the light was suddenly extinguished. It remained out for another full minute, then went on again.

STEVE THREW away his cigarette, and entered the apartment house. He avoided the elevator and went up the single flight of stairs to the first floor. At the door of Apartment 1A he pressed the button three times quickly, then twice, then once. The door was opened immediately, and he stepped inside.

The girl who met him in the foyer was so breathtakingly lovely that anyone who saw her once could never forget her. She was little more than nineteen. The white oval of her face was set off by dark, silky-soft hair. And her resemblance to Mary Watson was so marked that there could be no doubt she was the daughter of the woman who had died on Riverside Drive a few minutes ago.

Sue Watson said nothing as she closed the door behind Stephen Klaw. She just stood in the foyer, her slim and graceful body taut, her lower lip trembling. Her eyes bored deep into Steve's, as if she would delve into his very soul.

Suddenly, she closed her eyes, and a little moan escaped from her lips.

"Dead?" she asked. She opened her eyes and waited for the answer.

Stephen Klaw gulped, and bowed his head.

Sue Watson did not burst into tears. Her face became white, and her hands clenched at her sides. She swayed just a little, and Steve put forth a hand, then quickly withdrew it.

Silently, Sue Watson turned and led him into the living room. She went to the window, pulled the blind all the way down. Then she came and seated herself in a straight-backed chair facing Klaw.

"Tell me all about it, Steve," she said in a tight little voice. "I want to know how she died."

"She was a very brave woman, Sue," he told her. "She was mortally wounded, yet she managed to make her way to the place where she was to meet me. She brought the list of names— all but Trebizond's. We still don't know what name Trebizond adopted since coming to the United States."

Sue Watson's eyes widened. "Then—then she threw away her life! She died in vain?"

"No!" Steve told her grimly. "Your mother did not die in vain. We'll use that list to bring Trebizond out in the open. As soon as Kerrigan and Murdoch get here, we'll go into action. Have they called yet?"

"Yes. They called fifteen minutes ago from the airport. They'll be here any minute. But—but how can just the three of you fight the whole Skull and Swastika Corps? Won't the government help you at all?"

"No. We're on our own. We're acting as private citizens. Whatever we do is outside the law. There would be very little chance of getting enough evidence against the S.S. Corps to convict them in court. And even if we did, we couldn't afford to reveal our methods and our information at a public trial."

"I see," she said slowly. "So you three are going to stick your heads in the jackal's mouth—as usual!"

Klaw shrugged. "Your mother did it."

Twenty years ago, Mary Watson had been married to Franz Trebizond, who had even then been a member of the Nazi minority party in Germany. They had been divorced within a year, and Mary Watson had married again, and forgotten that nightmare year, during which she had learned just how much of a beast a man can be. When her second husband was killed in an airplane accident, Mary Watson had devoted her life to her two daughters, Sue and Eve. She had relegated Franz Trebizond to the limbo of forgotten things, had made a full life for herself in the busy duties of a mother.

But Franz Trebizond was not so easily disposed. In the intervening years he had risen to power with the Nazi party, and had become chief of the Bureau of Foreign Activity, directing Nazi spies and saboteurs from his headquarters in Berlin. Unfortunately, Mary Watson had not kept track of him. She had permitted Sue's elder sister, Eve, to make a vacation trip across Europe, just before the war broke out. Eve's itinerary had carried her through Berlin. And there, Eve had disappeared.

A WEEK later, Eve's body was found in the Danube River. Mary Watson, desperate with grief, began to pull wires and to seek information from friends in Europe. Little by little, she learned the story. Franz Trebizond had never forgotten her, never forgiven her for marrying another man and having two beautiful daughters by that other man. He had waited, and bided his time. It was he who had ordered Eve Watson's murder. And he had made sure that Mary Watson would hear of the circumstances.

There was nothing that Mary could do about it, until a few weeks ago. She learned that Franz Trebizond, who had directed Fifth Column activities in Holland, Belgium and South America, had come at last to the United States to take over the active direction of the Skull and Swastika Corps. She remembered that Trebizond had owned an old house in New York, and guessed that he might use it as headquarters. She had phoned Stephen Klaw, who was an old friend, that she would make an attempt to enter that house and obtain evidence. She had insisted, in spite of Steve's protests, that she wanted to do the job alone—as a gesture of vengeance for the murder of her daughter, Eve. And she had made the appointment to meet him at the spot where she had died tonight.

Now, looking at Sue Watson sitting straight and taut, Stephen Klaw remembered his promise to see that no harm came to this beautiful girl. There would be a double reason why the Skull and Swastika should go after her. The S.S. Corps was known for its ruthless acts of vengeance, even unto the second generation. And besides, the vindictiveness of Franz Trebizond would never be satisfied until he had wiped out the entire family of Mary Watson.

"You're sure," he asked her, "that this house is not being watched?"

"Quite sure," she told him, bitterly. "I've learned how to check on things like that. I wouldn't have given you the signal with the light if there had been any doubt. Mother and I have moved many times in the last years—always a little ahead of Trebizond. We cover our tracks."

Steve nodded. "Good. Then we can make our headquarters here—if you don't mind."

"If I don't mind!" Her eyes flashed. "Of course I don't! I want to help in the fight—" her voice broke—"for Eve's and Mother's sake!"

The telephone rang, and she sprang up to answer it. She spoke for a moment, then hung up and turned to Klaw.

"It's Johnny Kerrigan and Dan Murdoch. They're in the drug store around the corner. They're coming right up."

In less than five minutes, the bell rang, with the same signal that Klaw had used. Sue Watson went to the door and admitted Kerrigan and Murdoch.

They stepped swiftly inside, and grinned at Klaw. Klaw grinned back at them.

"Hello, mopes," he said.

"Hello, Shrimp," said Johnny Kerrigan.

"Hiya, Shrimp?" said Dan Murdoch.

These three had worked together for so long that they could almost read each other's minds. Long ago, they had found that they had one thing in common—a deliberate, willful, daredevil recklessness which made them always seek the longest odds and the most dangerous tasks. As Special Agents of the F.B.I., they were never assigned to routine jobs, but got only those assignments from which there was little chance of returning alive.

Stephen Klaw had once told the chairman of a senate investigating committee to go to hell when he had been asked why he shot to kill in a battle with a criminal gang. Johnny Kerrigan had once punched a senator's son in the nose. And Dan Murdoch had shot a crooked croupier to death in a gambling dive.

For such acts, any other agents would have been summarily dismissed from the Federal Bureau of Investigation. But the records of those three were so outstanding that they were allowed to retain their jobs—with this proviso: that they were never to be assigned to ordinary duty, where there might be a risk of offending the powers-that-be. They were kept in reserve for the undertakings for which the Chief of the F.B.I. would hesitate to order a man.

THAT WAS the way Kerrigan and Murdoch and Klaw wanted it. They were known as the Suicide Squad. Originally, there had been five of them. Then four. Now there were but three, and tomorrow there might be only two, one—or none. Only one thing was certain. If the Suicide Squad died, they would die fighting to the last gasp.

"You get all the breaks, Shrimp!" Johnny Kerrigan growled. "Dan and I were tied up in Washington, working on a secret code book that was found on a dead guy last week, while you had the excitement."

"How do you know I had excitement?" Steve demanded.

"I can see it in your eyes. And there are holes in your coat. They weren't made by moths!"

"Nice work," said Steve. "Keep at it, and you'll make a first-class detective some day."

Dan Murdoch came around and examined the holes in Steve's coat. Some of them were darkly flecked with congealed blood.

"Buckshot!" said Murdoch. "Take off your coat, Shrimp. We'll take out the pieces, and cauterize the holes. Do you want to get tetanus?"

Kerrigan chuckled. "The buckshot is more likely to get tetanus, if you ask me!"

Steve stripped off his coat and shirt, and Sue Watson went into the kitchen and boiled up a pot of water for sterilizing, and brought in gauze and scissors and a knife.

There were seven pellets in Klaw's body, and it was painful work removing them and cauterizing the small wounds. Kerrigan, for all his bulk, had marvelously sensitive fingers. It was he who did the work of extracting the lead, while Murdoch cauterized and bandaged.

While they labored over him, Steve told them swiftly what had happened on Riverside Drive, never even stopping to gasp when Dan applied a red-hot knife to the wounds.

He finished his story, and showed them the paper he had taken from Mary Watson's brief-case.

"If we could only work out this code!" he said. "We'd have the names of the Executive Council. It wouldn't give us Trebizond by a long shot, because I'm sure that even the Executive Council doesn't know the identity he's working under. But we could make use of those names—"

He stopped, seeing Kerrigan and Murdoch grinning at each other.

"What's the joke, mopes?"

"Oh, nothing," said Murdoch. He took the paper and went to a desk in the corner, turned on the light, and took a small notebook from his pocket. He began working with pencil and paper while Kerrigan finished up dressing Klaw's wounds.

In five minutes, Murdoch got up from the desk and came over with a sheet of paper upon which he had written nine names.

"Johnny told you we were working on a code book, didn't he? Well, we couldn't figure out which espionage organization was using that code. Now we know. The characters on this paper you got, are the same as the code book. It's the Skull and Swastika Code Book, and here's the list of names of their Executive Council!"

Steve took the paper eagerly. Kerrigan looked at the names over his shoulder, and whistled.

"Good Lord! They've got themselves in—solid!"

TWO OF the names were those of political bosses who controlled a large foreign vote. Four were city and state officials. The other three were fairly well-known business men of foreign extraction.

"We could arrest them all, tonight!" exclaimed Kerrigan.

"Sure!" Stephen Klaw barked. "And they'd be released in the morning for lack of evidence. This list wouldn't convict them in court. We'd only be putting Trebizond on guard!"

"Also," Murdoch added, "it is to be remembered that we are acting as private citizens, and not as Federal Agents." He grimaced. "No, my dear Mr. Kerrigan, your idea is putrid!"

"How'll we handle it then?" Johnny growled.

Stephen Klaw put his shirt and coat on, over his bandages.

"Watch me, mopes," he said. He turned to Sue Watson. "Is your phone on the dial system?"

She nodded. "Yes. Why—"

"Then they won't be able to trace the call back here."

He ran his finger down the list of names, and stopped at that of Sylvester Gröner.

"I've heard of him," Murdoch said. "He runs a travel bureau. Used to book personally conducted tours through Germany before the war."

"He'll do!" said Klaw. He went over to the telephone stand, looked up Gröner's home phone number, then dialed it.

Sue Watson looked blank and uncomprehending. But Kerrigan and Murdoch, after glancing at each other, nodded approval.

"Maybe you've got something there, Shrimp!" Dan Murdoch said.

Just then, Klaw got his connection. "Let mile talk to Mr. Gröner, please," he said. "My name? Just tell him it's Mr. Black—Mr. James Black…. No, Mr. Gröner doesn't know me. But he'll certainly be glad to talk to me."

Steve held the phone for a moment, winking at the others. Then he nodded as Sylvester Gröner's voice came over the wire.

"Yes?" they heard faintly. "What can I do for you?"

"Mr. Gröner," Steve said swiftly, "I know where to lay my hands on a certain list of names which was stolen from a certain place tonight. The government would give a handsome reward for that list, but I figure it's worth more to you. Say, a hundred thousand dollars."

There was a moment's silence, and they thought that Gröner had hung up. But then his voice was heard once more.

"Who are you?"

"You may call me Mr. Black. You can see I'm not bluffing, when I tell you that your name is number seven on the list."

"I don't know what you're talking about—"

"Suit yourself, Mr. Gröner. I'd just as soon turn the list over to the Government, unless I can make some money out of it. If you won't pay, why I'll just say good-by—"

"*Wait!*"

Steve held the wire, while there was another long pause. Then, "Just who are you, Mr. Black?"

"Let us say," Steve said into the phone, "that I represent an independent syndicate."

"International spies, eh?"

"Perhaps. Does it matter? Do you want to do business with me or not?"

"You say you have this list in your possession?"

"No. But I will get it tomorrow afternoon. I must know now whether you want to buy it. Otherwise, I will make other arrangements."

Gröner's voice was hesitant. "I must consult some one else. Give me an hour. Where can I get in touch with you?"

"You can't. But tomorrow, at exactly three-thirty in the afternoon, I'll register at the Groton Hotel. You can contact me there."

"You'll have the list with you?"

"No. But I'll be able to lay my hands on it, if you're ready to do business. And now—good-by, Mr. Gröner!"

He hung up swiftly, and turned to face the others. "Think he'll nibble, mopes?"

"Boy!" said Kerrigan. "I can just imagine how Gröner is burning up the wires right now, to get in touch with Franz Trebizond! Too bad we can't tap his wire!"

"Naughty, naughty!" said Dan Murdoch. "Mustn't do anything against the law!"

CHAPTER 3
ALIASES CAN'T FOOL DEATH

AT EXACTLY three-twenty the next afternoon, Stephen Klaw entered the lobby of the Groton Hotel. He had no baggage.

The lobby was busy, with people moving in and out of the cocktail lounge at the left. Klaw paid no attention to those who watched him as he passed. To all outward appearance, he might have been totally unaware that his every move was observed from the moment he stepped inside the door.

At the desk, he handed the clerk a ten dollar bill.

"Bath or shower, sir?" asked the clerk.

"Shower," said Steve. "And I want a room on an upper floor. Anything from the fifteenth up."

"So you can enjoy the view of Central Park, sir?"

"No," Steve told him. "I may have to throw some one out the window. I want him to have a long fall."

"Ha, ha," the clerk said nervously. "That's a good joke, sir." He took a key from the rack. "I can give you Room one-nine-one-o—"

"Okay." Klaw picked up the pen, and signed the register: *James Black, Washington, D.C.*"

While he was doing this, a woman in a black cloth coat with a chinchilla collar came over to the desk and idly picked a travel folder from the rack. She was a beautiful woman, with features so sharp and perfect that they might have been chiselled from Carrara marble by a master sculptor. Her gleaming yellow hair was arranged in a halo around her head, beneath a small chinchilla hat which matched the coat collar.

As she took the travel folder, her eyes darted across to the register, and rested for a fleeting instant upon the name which Stephen Klaw had signed. Then they flicked to the room number stamped upon the key, which the clerk was handing to a bellhop.

A faint smile, tinged with irony, tugged at her full red lips. She turned away from the desk and looked across the lobby, toward two men who were standing near the elevator. Her fingers appeared to be toying idly with the pearl necklace at her throat. In reality, they were moving in the swift gestures of the deaf-and-dumb sign language.

Stephen Klaw, *alias* Mr. James Black, seemed to be busy lighting a cigarette. But he did not miss the woman's actions, nor did he fail to take note of the two men to whom she was signalling. His face remained expressionless. Except for the sudden flicker of his slate-gray eyes, he gave no sign that he had noticed anything. But he saw those two men hurry into the elevator.

Without haste, he got his cigarette lit, accepted his change from the clerk, and then proceeded to compare his wrist watch with the electric clock over the desk. All this took only a couple of minutes. But it was long enough for the elevator cage containing those two men to reach its destination. Glancing at the indicator Steve saw that it had stopped at nineteen. The woman with the chinchilla collar moved across the lobby to the row of telephone booths alongside the entrance to the cocktail lounge. She entered one of them, and dialed a number, turning frequently to look back toward Steve.

Steve grinned. He glanced at the bellhop, who was waiting impatiently to take him upstairs.

"Just a minute, sonny," Steve said, and took the key out of the boy's hand. He put it down on the desk. "I've changed my mind," he told the clerk. "The nineteenth floor is a little too high. Have you got anything on the eighteenth?"

The clerk sighed. "Well, sir, there's nothing wrong with the nineteenth, but if you insist—" he replaced the key, and took another from the rack—"here's the corresponding room on the eighteenth floor."

"That's *much* better," Steve approved. Now he followed the boy over to the elevators. The cage which had taken the two men up was already descending, but there was another one waiting, and they entered it. As the operator slid the door shut, Steve got a quick, fleeting glimpse of the woman in the chinchilla-collared coat. She was hurrying out of the phone booth, and making a bee line for the desk, evidently in great excitement. She had left the telephone receiver dangling by the cord in the booth, indicating that she had not yet finished her conversation with whomever she had called. She must have sensed that Stephen

Klaw had pulled a fast one at the desk, and she was losing no time in checking up.

KLAW CHUCKLED. He saw the bellhop watching him, and he winked. The boy grinned, and winked back. Stephen Klaw was not the type to inspire fear or respect at first glance. He was so slim and wiry that he looked hardly older than the bellboy. It was only when one saw the cold glint in those slate-gray eyes of his that one must instantly realize he was no kid.

The elevator reached the eighteenth floor, and Klaw followed the uniformed lad down the carpeted hallway to 1810. The boy opened the door, and they went in. Klaw took out a five dollar bill and gave it to the lad.

"Gee, thanks, mister!" the kid gulped.

Klaw smiled. "This is just to show you who's your friend, sonny. Now scram. Things will be getting hot here pretty soon."

He fairly thrust the lad out of the room, and shut the door. But he was careful not to lock it.

He glanced at his wrist watch, and saw that it was exactly three o'clock. Almost at once, the telephone rang. He went to the night table and picked it up.

"James Black speaking," he said.

A familiar voice answered. "Hello, Mr. Black. This is Mr. White."

Steve grinned. Nobody who had ever heard that deep, stentorian voice of big Johnny Kerrigan could ever mistake it again for another. Kerrigan was the second of that triumvirate of daredevils who had come to be known in the F.B.I. as the Suicide Squad. The third was Dan Murdoch. Where one of them appeared, the other two were sure to be somewhere in the offing. They worked together like the well-oiled mechanism of a precision machine. The combination of Kerrigan, Murdoch and Klaw was one which the mightiest of felons had grown to fear.

Stephen Klaw chuckled into the phone. "How are you doing, Mr. White?"

"Not so bad, Mr. Black. I was behind that newspaper in the corner of the lobby when you came in. I watched the dame go in to phone. When she came dashing out, I stepped into the next booth, and traced the call. So now I know to whom she is reporting."

"Excellent work, Mr. White. Anything else?"

"Yeah. She scrammed back into her booth and finished up her conversation in a hurry, and then she phoned up to Room One-nine-one-o. She was so excited that I could hear what she said. She told the two bozos in there that you had switched rooms, and that they should go to Room Eighteen-ten and tackle you at once. They must be on the way down right now."

"Thanks, Mr. White. I've left my door unlocked for them."

"Watch yourself, Shrimp—"

"Nuts to you, Mr. White. Hang up, please. I expect a call from Mr. Green."

"Okay, Shrimp. Good-by."

Klaw put the phone down, glanced at his wrist watch, and waited at the telephone stand, with his back to the door. He kept his right hand dug deep down in his coat pocket, and his left was on the phone. His wrist watch showed four minutes after three.

He heard his doorknob creak slightly as it was tried from

outside, but he did not turn around. He kept his eyes on the second-hand of his watch. When it had made a complete revolution, bringing the time to three-five, the phone rang once more. He picked it up and said, "Mr. Black speaking."

"Hello, Mr. Black," came Dan Murdoch's voice. "This is Mr. Green. I have those papers for you. Will you meet me at the usual place?"

"Louder," said Stephen Klaw.

HE KNEW that the door was opening behind him, because he was standing in such a way that he could see the dresser mirror out of the corner of his eye. He glimpsed a long thin face, with a small moustache. It was the face of one of the two men who had been in the lobby and who had hurried up to Room 1910. The man was pushing the door carefully, squeezing his body through the opening. He had a small Smith & Wesson automatic pistol in his hand.

Steve took no notice. He held the French phone at his ear, and repeated, "Louder, Mr. Green."

Over the wire, Dan Murdoch's voice whispered, "Did they rise to the bait, Shrimp?"

"Yes."

"Are they in the room?"

"Yes."

"Okay, Shrimp, here goes." Murdoch raised his voice.

"THIS IS MR. GREEN," he shouted. "I HAVE THOSE PAPERS FOR YOU. IF YOU WILL MEET ME AT THE USUAL PLACE, I'LL DELIVER THEM TO YOU!"

"All right, Mr. Green. I'll meet you there in fifteen minutes. Good-by."

Stephen Klaw put the phone down, still with his right hand in his coat pocket. As if casually, he put his left hand in his other pocket. He turned around and faced the two men who had come into the room. Neither of them looked dangerous, except for the weapons in their hands. The first, with his small, well-kept moustache and thin, almost aristocratic face, might have been a banker or a director of a large corporation. The second was soft, and a bit paunchy, with a rotund, good-natured face, and could have passed for a genial neighborhood doctor.

The stout man pushed the door shut behind him with a poke of his elbow, while the one with the moustache bowed from the hips.

"Mr. Black," he said, in faultless, painstaking English which betrayed the fact that he was a foreigner of excellent education. "I must beg your pardon for this unceremonious entrance. But the urgency of our business with you must serve as an excuse. In *our* profession—" he jerked his head toward his stout companion, who beamed—"and in *yours*, there is a motto to the effect that the end justifies the means."

"I see," Stephen Klaw said drily. "And what is it you want?"

"I am so glad to see that you are a reasonable man, Mr. Black. Permit me to introduce myself. I am—Mr. Smith. And this—" nodding in the direction of the stout man—"is Mr. Jones."

"Very interesting," said Steve.

Mr. Smith and Mr. Jones both kept their automatics carefully pointed at Klaw's stomach.

"We just heard you making an appointment over the phone with a certain Mr. Green. You are going to meet him, and he is going to turn over to you a certain list of names. Not so?"

"You're doing the talking," Steve said noncommittally.

Mr. Smith shrugged. "Please do not make it hard for us. We know that your name is not Black, and that your friend's name is not Green, just as *you* know that our names are not Smith and Jones. Let us not beat around the bush. Mr. Jones and I are members of the S.S. Corps. You know, naturally, what the S.S. Corps represents?"

"Never heard of it," Steve lied, with a straight face.

Mr. Smith sighed. He looked sideways at Mr. Jones, taking care not to let his gun muzzle waver from Stephen Klaw's stomach.

"Show him just who we are, Mr. Jones."

The stout Mr. Jones showed all his teeth in a hearty, genial smile. "It will be a pleasure, indeed!"

Keeping his gun trained on Steve, he used his left hand to turn back the lapel of his coat. A glittering button was fastened to it.

"You will recognize this emblem, Mr. Black," he said, and moved up closer, thrusting the lapel out to bring the button nearer to Steve's eyes.

It was about the size of a quarter, and made of some sort of black, polished onyx. Upon its surface was carved a gleaming silver skull, and superimposed upon the skull there was a golden swastika.

"Ah," said Steve, acting as if a great light had just dawned upon him. "S.S.—Skull and Swastika. I recognize it now!"

"Exactly!" beamed Mr. Jones.

MR. SMITH stepped forward so that he was alongside of Mr. Jones. He pushed the muzzle of his gun up against Steve's diaphragm.

"It will do you no good to pretend ignorance, Mr. Black. We of the Skull and Swastika Corps are not fools. We know that you belong to the government, and that your real name is Stephen Klaw. We know that you have come here to contact a certain Mr. Green, whose real name is Murdoch. He is to turn over to you a list of the Executive Council of the S.S. Corps. We just heard you making an appointment to meet him."

Stephen Klaw kept his hands in his pockets, and gazed bleakly at those two.

"You're pretty well-informed, aren't you?"

"Extremely so. And we might as well tell you that we are prepared to go to any lengths to keep that list of names from falling into the hands of the United States Government."

"How far?"

Mr. Smith wiggled his gun, and shrugged. "Murder—*and further!*"

Steve raised his eyebrows. "What's further than murder?"

Mr. Smith gestured impatiently with his automatic. "Please don't waste time. Surely you remember the newspaper stories of the girl who was found last week with her tongue cut out, and—"

"I remember," Steve said hastily. There was a queer, flickering light in his eyes. "That was Estelle Frazer. She had just come back from Germany, and she was scheduled to appear before a Senate Investigating Committee, to tell certain secrets she had learned there."

"Quite so," said Mr. Smith. "But she never talked. She begged to be killed quickly, Mr. Black. There have been others, too."

Stephen Klaw's eyes were no longer flickering. They were cold and hard. His hands, still dug deep in his pockets, were motionless. He asked quietly—almost too quietly: "So it was you two gentlemen who tortured her, and then left her mutilated body to be found?"

Mr. Jones beamed. "Exactly, exactly. It served as an example of the power of the Skull and Swastika Corps. Now you, Mr. Klaw, can save yourself a great deal of bodily pain by disclosing to us the place where you were to meet Mr. Green. We will go instead, and relieve him of the list."

"And what happens to me?" Klaw asked.

"As soon as we have the list safe," Mr. Jones promised unctuously, "we will let you go."

"You lie," said Stephen Klaw. "You've just confessed to me that you tortured and murdered Estelle Frazer. You can't afford to let me live."

Mr. Jones was about to protest, but Mr. Smith stopped him. He nodded sympathetically at Steve.

"That is true. The best we can promise you is a quick death. Speak now, and tell us where you are to meet Murdoch, and we will kill you mercifully with a bullet. If you refuse, we will have to—ah—make your last hours on earth a nightmare of agony. Do not doubt that we can do it. We have already told you about

171

Estelle Frazer. There have been others. We have men downstairs in the lobby, whom we can bring up. They have all the necessary paraphernalia. We will hang out a 'Do Not Disturb' sign, and proceed to work on you at our leisure."

"That," said Stephen Klaw, "is all I wanted to know!"

"What do you mean?" demanded Mr. Smith. "Do you mean that you will talk—"

"No," said Steve. "I mean that I will shoot!"

He fired both automatics in his coat pockets, without removing them. He merely thrust the muzzles up as far as they would go, and pulled the triggers. The bullets scorched the cloth of his coat. The explosions were low, muffled. The slugs—one from each gun—struck Mr. Smith and Mr. Jones as accurately as if he had aimed carefully and painstakingly. He got each of them in the right arm, just above the elbow.

And then, a very curious thing happened. Steve had aimed deliberately at the gun arm of both men, because he knew that they would pull the triggers of their own weapons, even if only by reflex action. He had hoped that the driving force of his own shots would swing them around, so that he would not be hit. IN THIS he was correct. But Mr. Smith, who was standing at the right of Mr. Jones, was whirled around in such fashion that his back was turned to the stout and genial Mr. Jones.

Both guns went off at almost the same instant, echoing Steve's two shots. Mr. Smith's shot went harmlessly into the wall, but Mr. Jones's slug smashed squarely into Mr. Smith's back.

Mr. Smith toppled forward, blood gushing from his mouth.

He fell against the wall, then slid to the floor, and remained there, motionless.

Mr. Jones gazed at his dead confrere, as if spellbound. His right arm hung limp at his side, and the automatic which had driven and killed Smith fell from his numbed hand. He uttered a choked cry of rage, and stopped to pick up the gun with his left hand.

Stephen Klaw sighed, and hit him once behind the ear with the butt of his reversed automatic.

The stout Mr. Jones fell across the body of Mr. Smith.

Steve bent and pulled the unconscious Jones off the body of Smith, and maneuvered around till he got the man's coat off. Jones's arm was bleeding profusely. Steve didn't bother to stop and examine it. He went to the bed and yanked a sheet off, tore it into strips, and tied it as tightly as he could around Jones's arm, above the wound, in the form of a rough tourniquet. Then, to make sure that Mr. Smith would not wake up and go away from there, Steve handcuffed him to the bed.

He went methodically through the pockets of both men, removing everything he found, including the black-laquered Skull-and-Swastika buttons. He had just about finished, when the telephone rang again.

He picked it up, and was greeted by Johnny Kerrigan's voice.

"Hello, Mr. Black, how you doing?"

"I'm doing all right, Mr. White. I had two visitors."

"How do they feel now?"

"One of them is past all feeling. The other isn't interested. I have two of the buttons."

"Very nice work, Mr. Black. Come on down. The lady with the yellow hair and the chinchilla collar is getting restless. I can see her from the phone booth here, and she's biting her fingernails."

"Is she alone?"

"Not much. There's at least half a dozen bozos in here that are taking orders from her. Those two you interviewed upstairs were only a scouting force."

Steve grinned. "I'll be right down!"

He hung up and hurried out of the room. On the way he picked up the "Do Not Disturb" sign, and hung it on the knob. He made sure the door was locked, and went down the hall to the elevator. Once more he slipped both hands into his coat pockets....

CHAPTER 4
BROKEN PROMISE

THE LOBBY was just as busy as it had been ten minutes ago, but with this difference—there was an air of tense expectancy which somehow seemed to charge the atmosphere with latent dynamite.

Stepping out of the elevator, Stephen Klaw threw a swift, comprehensive glance around, seeking to orientate himself to all the focal points of danger. He spotted Johnny Kerrigan, still in the telephone booth, engrossed in a mythical conversation over the wire. Johnny had his lips close to the mouthpiece, with the receiver at his ear, and was going through all the motions of talking, but he was in reality keeping a sharp weather eye out on the occupants of the lobby.

Johnny nodded almost imperceptibly in the direction of the cocktail lounge, and Steve looked in that direction and saw the tall, slender figure of Dan Murdoch, seated at the bar in there and sipping his inevitable Scotch-and-soda. From where Murdoch sat he had a clear view of the lobby, and there was nothing between him and the hotel foyer to obstruct the possible line of fire in the event of trouble.

Murdoch winked over his highball glass, but Steve Klaw did not return the wink.

Steve got that much of the picture as he stepped out of the elevator cage. Next, he switched to the lobby itself.

The yellow-haired woman with the chinchilla collar was seated in an easy chair, with her long silk-stockinged legs crossed, smoking a cigarette through a thin ivory holder. When she saw Steve, she almost dropped the holder. She started to get up. Then she let herself sink back into the chair as she saw Stephen Klaw coming straight across the lobby toward her.

Steve had his hands in his pockets. He was walking slowly, deliberately. He had spotted at least a half dozen men in the lobby, who looked as if they might be the ones to whom Kerrigan had referred when he said that the woman had more help at hand. There were two near the cigar counter, two at the desk, and one apiece at the elevator doors and at the street entrance. Whether or not there were more, he could not tell. But after the first quick glance of reconnaissance, he did not look again in the direction of those men. His whole attention was centered upon the woman, for he was sure that nothing would happen here until she gave the signal.

He stopped squarely in front of her and looked down, smiling. For a brief, fleeting moment, he glimpsed a flicker of emotion in her eyes. Whether it was fear, hate or consternation, he could not tell. Then she dropped long-lashed lids to veil her eyes. She returned his smile. She took a long puff of the cigarette through the ivory holder, and allowed the smoke to trickle out through pursed lips.

"How do you do, Mr.—er—Black?" she said in a low, throaty voice.

"Good afternoon, Lisa Monterey," Stephen Klaw said levelly.

A quick spasm of surprise passed across her cameo features. The long fingers on the ivory cigarette holder tautened.

"You know my name?"

"Of course. We've known for a long time that you were an agent of the Skull and Swastika Corps. In fact, the F.B.I. knows almost as much about you as you do, yourself. For instance, we know that you worked for two years in the Balkans as an agent of the Nazis, under the notorious Franz Trebizond. Then, when Trebizond went to South America, you accompanied him. Now that Trebizond has been ordered to the United States to direct Fifth Column activities, you are his chief lieutenant. We even have a list of all the aliases you've used. In Rumania, you were Dora Caminescu. In Holland, you were Maria Nordlung. In Paraguay, you were Lisa Monterey. You kept that last name when you came here, because it was too difficult to get another passport."

176

She was leaning forward in her chair now, staring at him. "Do you know the name my chief is using in America?"

"Franz Trebizond? No. We don't know yet. But give us a little more time. We've just started to work on the Skull and Swastika Corps."

Her lips curled scornfully. "You are a fool for telling me all this, Mr.—er—Black. If I am really in the employ of Franz Trebizond, as you imply, what is to prevent me from warning him at once?"

"Nothing," Steve told her grimly. "In fact, I want you to warn him. I want you to give him a message from me—Stephen Klaw."

SLOWLY, SHE arose from the chair. Standing, she was almost regal in carriage and manner. But there was a certain nervous tension about her, which Steve detected from the rapid heaving of her breast.

"I admit nothing. You are only talking for the purpose of trapping me into an admission. Then you would arrest me."

"On the contrary," Steve said, grinning. "I could arrest you now, upon the evidence I have. It was you who sent those two pleasant gentlemen up to interview me in Room Eighteen-ten. That's enough to hold you on. But it isn't you I want. It's Franz Trebizond. Go and tell him that Stephen Klaw gives him twenty-four hours to get out of the country!"

Lisa Monterey laughed. "You talk very big, Mr. Stephen Klaw. But what can you do? You don't even know where Franz Trebizond is to be found. You don't know what name he uses in this country."

"I'll know all that before midnight," he told her. "One of the two kind gentlemen who visited me upstairs, is still alive. He told me how he intended to make *me* talk. I'll use the same method with him. And it will work!"

The woman's eyes flashed. "You are wrong, Mr. Stephen Klaw," she murmured. "Oh, you are very wrong. You will make no one talk. *You are practically a dead man now!*"

As she finished talking, she sprang away from Klaw, and began to run toward the street entrance. At the same time she did something with her finger to the ivory cigarette holder, and then applied it to her lips. She blew a great gust of breath into it, and the shrill note of a whistle emanated from the holder.

That whistle was the signal for which her men had been waiting. As if magically, guns appeared in their hands, the muzzles swinging with murderous certainty to center upon the slim figure of Stephen Klaw.

He did not turn to run, neither did he seek cover.

There was a faint smile upon his lips as both his hands came out of the jacket pockets, the two automatics barking in a rhythmic melody of doom. He held them close to his hips, firing from that position. He did not shoot with frantic speed or with jerky desperation, as a man might be expected to do when he is attacked by superior numbers. Instead, he fired each shot deliberately, carefully, never missing. He swivelled slowly, as lead whined past his head. His first two shots caught the two men at the desk, and then he turned his fire on those at the cigar counter. He paid no attention to the one at the street entrance or to the one at the elevator doors.

178

He had no need to, for they were being well taken care of by Dan Murdoch, who had come out of the cocktail lounge with both his heavy revolvers spitting and roaring.

The hotel lobby reverberated to the thunder of deadly gunfire, and the rolling clouds of sound echoed back from the walls and ceiling with the shattering force of a volcanic eruption.

Screams of frightened women, and the hoarse shouts of frantic men formed a ghastly chorus to the deep-throated roar of the guns. Patrons ran about blindly, seeking safety from the whistling, shrieking leaden bolts of death. A man, nicked in the ear by a stray bullet, clapped both hands to his head and shouted that he was dying.

In a matter of moments, the bustling, peaceful lobby was transformed into an inferno of terror and panic. Those six gunmen of the Skull and Swastika Corps lay dead on the floor. The shooting was over, but the panic grew. A milling, seething throng of men and women fought to gain the exits.

Stephen Klaw remained standing for a moment in the middle of the lobby, watchful for the appearance of other gunmen. Dan Murdoch, tall and lithe, stood poised in the doorway of the cocktail lounge, a smoking revolver in each hand. The two of them glanced across at each other, and they both nodded. The battle was over. Murdoch sheathed his revolvers; Klaw slipped his hot automatics back into his coat pockets. They both turned to look for Kerrigan.

In that shouting, stampeding throng, they could not find him. He was no longer in the telephone booth. There was no sign of him anywhere.

Neither was there any sign of Lisa Monterey!

POLICE WHISTLES were keening shrilly, outside. A siren was shrieking somewhere, and rapidly approaching.

Klaw slid through the throng, and reached Murdoch's side.

"Let's go, mope," he said. "We don't want to answer any police questions now!"

"What about Johnny?" Murdoch asked.

"He must have tailed the Monterey woman out of here. That was his end of the job. Let's move fast. We have a little job of our own to attend to upstairs!"

Dan Murdoch followed him through the lobby to the rear, then down a flight of stairs to the service basement. They found an elevator here, deserted by its operator, who had no doubt left his post to see the excitement upstairs.

Klaw and Murdoch got into it, and Steve sent the cage scooting up to the eighteenth floor. He unlocked the door of 1810, and pointed silently to the prostrate form of the stout Mr. Jones, who was just recovering consciousness from the blow on the head. Jones was still groggy, and hardly knew what was happening to him as Klaw unlocked the handcuffs fastening him to the bed.

It was mute testimony to the efficiency with which the Suicide Squad worked together, that no word of explanation or instruction was necessary between Klaw and Murdoch now. Murdoch knelt and slung the stout man over his shoulder, and then followed Steve out of the room. Steve closed the door once more, leaving the "Do Not Disturb" sign on the knob, so that the body of Mr. Smith would not be found for a while. Then they made their way down the corridor back to the service elevator.

Down in the basement, Klaw went out first, reconnoitering the lay of the land. There was no one down here, but they could hear the shouts of the police up above, trying to quiet the panic-stricken crowd in the lobby, and find out just what had happened.

Steve whistled for Murdoch to follow him, and made his way to the back of the basement where there was a loading platform for trunks and baggage. Outside the platform stood a hotel station wagon, empty.

Murdoch dumped the stout Mr. Jones into the rear, and cuffed him to the doorframe. Then he and Klaw climbed into the cab, with Klaw behind the wheel. The key was in the switch, ready for the next trip, and Klaw grinned as he turned it on.

"It's nice of the Hotel Groton to provide an easy getaway like this for us!"

"Lay off the jabber and get going, Shrimp," Dan Murdoch growled. "The police will be around here in a minute." Klaw nodded, and stepped on the starter. He gave her the gas, and they rolled out of the alley into the street.

A great crowd was collected fifty feet up the block, in front of the hotel entrance. No one even noticed the station wagon as it turned left to the corner, and swung north on Broadway.

Klaw drove slowly, without making any effort to throw off possible pursuit.

"The bird in back," he told Murdoch, "gave the name of Jones. He's an agent of the Skull and Swastika Corps, and he's one of the devils who tortured poor Estelle Frazer before they killed her."

"Ah!" said Dan Murdoch.

"Our job," Klaw went on, "is to get the Skull and Swastika Corps to come out in the open. So far, we've done pretty good. They fell hook, line and sinker for the story that I was to pick up a list of the allies of their executive council. But this is only the beginning. If we can't bring Franz Trebizond out into the open, we fail. I figure that by holding on to Mr. Jones, we can do it."

Murdoch nodded. "Trebizond will be afraid that Jones may talk. And he'll try to get him out of our hands."

"Or knock him off. Either way, it's Trebizond's move next."

"Unless my eyesight fails me," Dan Murdoch said, looking to the left, past Steve, "Trebizond is making his next move already!"

Steve glanced out of his window, and saw what Murdoch meant.

A long, two-toned town car had drawn abreast of them. The lower part of the body was black, the upper, maroon. A uniformed chauffeur was at the wheel, and a second man in uniform sat beside him. In the rear of the car were two more men, and a woman.

A SINGLE glance was enough to tell Steve Klaw that the woman was Lisa Monterey. Though he was not able to distinguish her features in the interior of the car, he spotted the light chinchilla collar and the silver chinchilla hat. She was sitting on the far side of the seat. One of the men was seated beside her, and the other occupied a folding seat just in front of her. This latter one was holding a small, sawed-off sub-machine gun, with the foreshortened muzzle poking out of the window straight at Klaw. His face was down low, sighting along the barrel, and his finger was on the trip.

Those particular weapons had never been used in the United States until introduced by the Skull and Swastika Corps. The infernal Franz Trebizond had brought them over with him, and they proved a most effective means of terrorization. Anyone who was inclined to inform against the Skull and Swastika was sure to change his mind when he read how the victims of those sawed-off shotguns lived for two or three days, enduring the most agonizing of torture from the multitudinous wounds, and then dying.

The second man, seated beside Lisa Monterey, had another of the vicious weapons, which he was aiming from inside the the car. The careful planning which had gone into this attack was evident—for the two machine-gunners were so placed that it was almost impossible to shoot them both at the same time. If, by some miracle, Klaw or Murdoch should succeed in hitting one of them, the other could pull the trigger of his machine-gun, riddling them both with the same burst.

Klaw took in the situation at a glance, as Murdoch whispered fiercely, "They've got us cold, Shrimp. But Johnny's supposed to be tailing that dame."

Klaw nodded, gripping the wheel. The limousine was swiftly pulling ahead of them, bringing the two machine-gunners directly abreast of Klaw and Murdoch. In another moment, they would be in position to fire.

Stephen Klaw stepped all the way down on the gas, and the

station wagon spurted forward. Luckily, there wasn't much traffic on Broadway at this time of the afternoon, and there was a clear lane ahead. But the chauffeur of the limousine had been watching for just such a move, and he matched Steve's effort. The limousine thrust forward, and started to gain on the station wagon.

The two cars sped up Broadway with roaring exhausts, in a death-race. There was hardly twelve inches of space between them as the long snout of the limousine began to edge out in front of the station wagon, bringing the machine-gunners slowly and surely into firing position. Ahead glowed a red traffic light, and a police officer at the corner was madly waving a hand to them to stop, while he tugged his revolver out with the other.

Dan Murdoch had a gun in each hand now, but he couldn't get in position to fire past Steve at the machine-gunners. Everything depended now on whether Klaw could keep the station wagon from falling another foot behind the limousine. He was keeping his eyes fixed on the street ahead, driving with every facility alert, and feeding her every ounce of gas that she would take. They flashed past the corner, and the cop jumped out of the way just in the nick of time. Then the two cars were racing up toward Columbus Circle, neck-and-neck, but with the limousine gaining by inches—and inches were all it needed.

Murdoch's dark and handsome face was set and grim. He swung around in the seat, and leaned far back, stretching his left arm out behind Steve's head to aim at one of the machine-gunners. But the wooden panelling of the station wagon was so high that it shut off his view of those two. There was no way for him to get at them until they came up abreast of the cab, and by then it would be too late.

Quietly he said, "I'm stymied, Shrimp. You'll have to crash them."

IT WAS typical of the utter confidence they had in each other, that Klaw asked no further questions, taking it for granted that what Murdoch said was so. Crashing that other car was the last thing in the world they wanted. It would mean surrendering their prisoner to the police, for they could never hope to spirit him away from an accident on Broadway, as they had from the Groton Hotel.

Their orders from Washington had been strict. They must operate as an independent army of three, a sort of private Blitz-krieg against the Skull and Swastika Corps. They must not seek the help of the local police, or of the local F.B.I. office. Nothing they did could be official, for the diplomatic repercussions would be beyond calculation.

Besides, the Skull and Swastika Corps was known to have tentacles reaching into many key posts in the police and judiciary. Not so long ago, an important public servant had felt impelled to go on the radio to deny rumors that he was sympathetic to the S.S. Corps. As a matter of fact, that official was a loyal American of French extraction, who hated the Skull and Swastika, and everything it stood for. But he had a father, mother, two sisters and a brother in occupied France, and he knew that if he did not obey orders from Franz Trebizond, his relatives would be tortured mercilessly. So, once the stout Mr.

Jones fell into the hands of the police, there was a good chance that Trebizond might get him out of custody.

That was why the Suicide Squad had been assigned to this job. If they came to grief on this assignment, there would be no support for them from the Department of Justice. They would be disowned, and they would swear up and down that they had been acting in a private capacity, and not as agents of the United States Government.

All this was in the mind of Stephen Klaw as he twisted the wheel to crash the station wagon into the limousine. And he knew that it was also in the mind of Dan Murdoch. But he knew too, that Murdoch would never have ordered it unless it were supremely necessary. Therefore, he complied without question.

The two cars met with a crashing, rending sound of tearing metal as the left front fender of the station wagon tore into the right fender of the limousine. Both cars swerved out over to the southbound lane, but neither stopped. The chauffeur of the limousine was pouring gas into his motor, just as Stephen Klaw was doing, each making a supreme effort to pull ahead of the other. The purpose of the limousine was to bring those sawed-off machine-guns abreast of Klaw and Murdoch, while Steve's purpose was to get as far ahead as possible, to be out of range of the vicious weapons, and to give Murdoch a chance to use his revolvers.

The Broadway crowd, rendered blasé by years of stunt attractions calculated to pry it loose from its money, was treated to the free spectacle of a tug-of-war between two automobiles, with death as the prize for the loser.

The cars were locked together inextricably by their fenders, and it became evident in a moment that neither could pull ahead of the other. Klaw and Murdoch realized this at the same moment as the killers in the limousine. The yellow-haired Lisa Monterey screamed to her two gunners to shoot, and the men thrust their murderous machine-guns far out of the window, with their fingers on the trips. They were going to blast through the partition of the station wagon.

Dan Murdoch smashed the glass behind the driver's seat, and literally leaped through into the tonneau, landing on hands and knees. Then he was up in a split-second, both his revolvers thundering.

He fired six times swiftly with each gun at point-blank range into the faces of the two machine-gunners, at the same time that Steve Klaw, abandoning the wheel, leaned far out of his window and began to pump both his automatics.

It is doubtful whose slugs killed those machine-gunners first. Klaw had inserted new clips in his automatics, and he emptied nine shots from each into the killers, while Murdoch fired twelve times with his two revolvers. And neither of them missed with a single shot.

THE FACES of the two machine-gunners disintegrated under that blasting barrage. And at the same time, Lisa Monterey opened the far door of the limousine and stepped out into the street. She lifted up her dress and dashed away. Her chauffeur and footman also took to their heels.

Klaw and Murdoch saw her go, but they were unable to stop her. Their guns were empty, and by the time they could get out of the station wagon and take after her, she would have plenty of time to disappear in the crowd. Lisa Monterey was making good her escape!

But now, another factor entered the picture. The big, hulking figure of Johnny Kerrigan came leaping out of a taxicab fifty feet behind, and made after the yellow-haired woman. He overtook her in a half dozen strides.

That was all Klaw and Murdoch had a chance to see. Their own position was precarious. The traffic cop was running up from the corner, and a crowd was beginning to form, which would cut off all escape for them. The prisoner could no longer be kept. They must leave him to the police.

"I say we scram out of here, Shrimp!" Murdoch yelled, above the clamor of the throng and the eddying echo of the gunfire.

Steve nodded. They both leaped out of the station wagon, and ran headlong into the gathering crowd, away from the approaching cop.

The crowd melted away from them at sight of their guns. Klaw and Murdoch were the only ones who knew that those guns were empty.

They reached the opposite sidewalk, with the cop shouting behind them, and afraid to shoot lest he hit an innocent bystander.

"Down there!" shouted Steve, pointing to the subway kiosk at the corner.

They both dived down the stairs, as the thunderous rumble of a local subway train sounded, rolling into the station below. Klaw, in the lead, hurdled the turnstiles without paying his nickel, and Dan Murdoch followed at his heels. They made the train by a half second, and heard the door slam shut behind them. The train started to move, and they turned and looked out at the sweating, cursing cop who came tearing into the station after them.

At the next local station they got out and raced up the stairs to the street, hailing a taxicab and pulling away only a moment before the siren of an approaching police car sounded, a block away. The alarm had gone out fast, but they had beaten it by the margin of a matter of seconds.

They left their cab after riding it three or four blocks, and took another. They changed cabs three times before they ventured to approach the neighborhood of Sue Watson's apartment house. In the last cab they reloaded their guns, then dismissed the taxi two blocks away and walked the rest of the distance.

The light was on in the first floor window, and the blind was down.

Steve nudged Dan Murdoch, and they kept on walking past the house, without displaying any interest.

"I don't like it, Dan," Steve Klaw said. "She's supposed to keep her shade up—except when one of us is up there."

"We better snap it up then!" Murdoch barked.

They turned into the garage next door, and Steve waved the attendant away.

"I just want to get something out of my car," he said. They went all the way to the rear of the garage, found the back exit, and stepped out into the concrete yard. From there they made their way into the yard of the apartment house, and went down to the basement.

THEY TOOK the back stairs up to the first floor, and Murdoch tried the door while Stephen Klaw waited, pressing his body against the corridor wall.

The door opened under Murdoch's touch, revealing the foyer. A man with a sawed-off machine-gun was standing in the foyer, with the muzzle of the deadly weapon trained upon the doorway.

"Good afternoon!" the man said to Murdoch, leering over the muzzle of the machine-gun. "We thought that some of the girl's friends would be coming to visit her. Put your hands up, and come right in!"

Dan Murdoch stood stiffly in the doorway, without moving. Steve Klaw was almost at his elbow, but was standing in such a way that he was not visible to the man with the gun. Murdoch smiled genially, but did not raise his hands. For the benefit of Klaw, he described the situation as best he could.

"So you're a Skull and Swastika man, eh? Waiting to shoot me down, eh? What did you do with Sue Watson?"

"She's been taken away, my friend," the gunman said. "She'll be well taken care of. As for you, come right in. We want to talk to you."

A second gunman appeared from the interior of the apartment, at the first one's elbow.

"See what I have caught, Hans!" the first one said over his shoulder to the second. "A nice big fish for our net!"

That was all he said. Stephen Klaw, at the first hint of trouble, had dropped to his knees and drawn both his automatics. He swung around on his knees, in front of the doorway, and peered up at the two gunmen in the foyer from between Murdoch's legs.

"You guys talk too much!" he said disgustedly.

The gunmen, startled, glanced down, swinging the muzzles of their machine-guns down to bear upon Klaw.

And Klaw fired from the ground, once with each automatic. He shot at an upward angle of about thirty degrees, but his aim was just as good as in level shooting. His slugs got both killers square in the throat, and sent them crashing back into the apartment with their machine-guns unfired.

The two explosions of his automatics sounded more like the backfire of an automobile than like pistol shouts.

"Nice work, Shrimp!" Murdoch said, and sprang forward into the apartment, drawing both his revolvers. He leaped over the still-thrashing bodies of the gunmen, into the living room. A third man was in there, methodically searching the place, with all the thoroughness of the Gestapo. The sofa had been ripped apart, the disemboweled cushions lay on the floor. The drawers of the desk had been pulled out and ransacked.

The man uttered a guttural curse and yanked out a pistol. Murdoch coolly shot him through the heart. Then he turned and looked at Stephen Klaw.

"Well, Shrimp," he said. "It looks like we didn't keep your promise to Mary Watson!"

Stephen Klaw's face was white. He gripped those two automatics tightly, as if he wished to beat some one's brains out with them.

"We've got to find her, Dan," he whispered. "We've got to find her—before they go to work on her!"

"Let's get out then," said Murdoch. "We'll never find her here!"

CHAPTER 5
THE LAIR OF TREBIZOND

STIFFLY, THEY walked out of the apartment, never looking at the dead men they left behind. They walked down the stairs and out into the street, like two automatons. They were both thinking of Sue Watson in the hands of Franz Trebizond. And they were remembering the things that had been done to Estelle Frazer, and to others who had fallen into those hands.

"Maybe," Dan Murdoch said hopefully, "maybe they left other men outside, to watch for us. Maybe they'll try to get us—"

"We've got to take the next one alive," Steve murmured. "We've got to make him tell us where to find Sue!"

He stopped as an automobile horn sounded across the street.

Both of them swivelled to face that sound, going for their guns. But they didn't draw them.

Murdoch said, "Ah!" and Klaw exhaled a great gust of breath.

It was a taxicab horn which was being blown across the street. The driver was using it to signal them, at the order of one of the occupants.

The occupants were Johnny Kerrigan and Lisa Monterey.

Swiftly they crossed the street and climbed into the cab.

Lisa Monterey's wrists were handcuffed behind her. She was sitting silent and sullen, next to Kerrigan, who was grinning. The taxicab driver turned around and winked as Murdoch and Klaw got in.

"Boys," said Kerrigan, nodding in the direction of the driver, "I want you to meet Sam Meyers, who hates the Skull and Swastika Corps as much as we do. I caught up with Miss Monterey here, and gave her the choice of coming along with me, or of being turned in to the police on a murder rap. P.S.—she preferred to come with me. Then I explained to Sam what it was all about, and he offered the use of his cab. So here we are."

"That's right, gents," Sam Meyers said eagerly. "Anything I can do to keep the Nazis outta this country—I'll do it. And I ain't afraid o' no fast action, neither. I was a corporal in the last war, an' seen plenty o' action—an' mud!"

"Glad to know you, Sam," said Dan Murdoch.

Steve Klaw turned to Kerrigan and said flatly, "Johnny, the skunks have got Sue!"

Kerrigan scowled, and nodded. "I thought so, when we drove up and saw the shade down."

Lisa Monterey smiled thinly. "You three men are fools. You can never beat the Skull and Swastika. Franz Trebizond will get you, as he has gotten all of the enemies of our Führer."

Steve Klaw, sitting backward on one of the folding chairs next to Murdoch, looked at her speculatively.

"You could tell us where they've got Sue Watson, couldn't you?"

She threw him a glance of vicious spite. "I will tell you nothing!"

Steve looked at Kerrigan. "When this dame phoned in to her headquarters from the lobby of the Hotel Groton, Johnny, you checked on the call?"

"I did," said Johnny. "I got the number, and traced the address through the telephone company. But it was a blind lead, Steve. That address is the home of Judge Hinchley. There must be some mistake. Judge Hinchley was a Congressman before he was appointed Judge, and he introduced a bill in Congress to force the deportation of every alien member of the Skull and Swastika Corps."

"I see," Steve said thoughtfully. He had been watching Lisa Monterey keenly as Johnny spoke, and he saw the sudden involuntary jerk of her shoulders at the mention of Judge Hinchley. Her eyes widened almost imperceptibly, and then were immediately veiled.

"Suppose we go see Judge Hinchley," he said. "Perhaps some servant in the Judge's home is acting as intermediary for Trebizond. The servant may be a clearing house for messages between agents of the Skull and Swastika."

"Let's go!" said Johnny Kerrigan.

THE JUDGE'S home was a low, rambling Colonial, built on a large, landscaped plot of ground in Riverdale, just within the city limits. It was a good forty minute drive from where they started, but Sam Meyer made it in twenty minutes flat.

They parked a hundred feet away, and left Lisa Monterey

handcuffed to the door-frame of the cab, in the charge of Sam Meyer.

Stephen Klaw went up the flower-bordered walk to the front door, while Kerrigan and Murdoch faded into the shrubbery surrounding the house.

A burly manservant answered the bell, and scowled at Steve.

"May I see Judge Hinchley?" Steve asked mildly.

The manservant filled the doorway, towering above Klaw.

"I'm sorry," he said gruffly. "Judge Hinchley has been ill with a heart attack, for the past month. He can see no one."

"I'm sure he'll want to see me," Steve said, "if you'll take my name in to him. The name is—Black."

He watched the man's face, but caught no reaction. He went on swiftly, stabbing in the dark. "It's all right, you can take me in to the Chief. I was sent here by Lisa Monterey."

Now he saw the man's eyes flicker. But he recovered his stolid pose at once. "I don't know that name. But step in. I'll tell Mr. Belding, the Judge's secretary."

The man moved aside, and Steve stepped inside, sliding his hands into his coat pockets.

The servant led him into a waiting room at the side of the foyer, and left him there. Steve did not sit down. He stood with his back to the window, and tapped gently upon the pane with his fingernail. An answering tap sounded from outside. It was either Johnny Kerrigan or Dan Murdoch.

Steve ran his fingertips along the window sash and found the wire of a burglar-alarm system. Swiftly he felt along the wire, until he came to a spot where the wire had been spliced into the main burglar alarm line. He twisted at the tape, ripped it off, and separated the two wires. He tapped once again on the pane, and stepped away from the window just as the door opened and a stocky, baldheaded man entered the room.

"I am Mr. Belding," said the baldheaded man. "Judge Hinchley's secretary. What can I do for you?"

Steve's hands were back in his pockets. "I've got to see the Judge," Steve said. "I have reason to believe that some one in this house is connected with the Skull and Swastika Corps."

Belding almost jumped under the sudden impact of that bleak statement.

"Impossible!" he exclaimed. "We are all loyal Americans in this house!"

"Nevertheless," Steve persisted, "there is at least one Skull and Swastika member here. Maybe more. I insist on seeing the Judge."

Belding looked at him queerly. "You said something to the butler about having been sent here by a woman named Lisa Monterey?"

"Yes."

"Who is this woman?"

"I'll tell the Judge when I see him."

Belding smiled thinly. "I'm sure you will. Follow me."

He turned and opened the door by which he had entered, and led the way through into the next room. Stephen Klaw entered, and stopped short on the threshold. His eyes widened momentarily.

This room was a library. But it was immense. The ceiling had been removed, making the room the height of the house, with a balcony running around all four sides. There were bookshelves both below and above the balcony. And hanging from the opposite was a great purple banner with the ghastly insignia of the Skull and Swastika. Standing up there on the balcony, in front of the banner, were four men in the natty uniform of the S.S. Corps. Each of them had a sawed-off machine-gun, which was trained upon Klaw.

Steve gave them only one glance, then centered his attention upon the long table at the other end of the room.

Sue Watson was seated at that table. Her wrists were handcuffed to the chair. A few feet away, there was another chair, in which was seated Judge Hinchley. Steve recognized him at once, but was startled by the change in the man. The Judge's face was haggard and pinched, and his eyes were deep-sunken wells of misery and shame. He sat half slumped in the chair in an attitude which bespoke utter hopelessless.

Behind the chair in which Sue Watson was handcuffed, stood Franz Trebizond.

STEPHEN KLAW had never seen the man, but he had gotten a good description from Mary Watson. Even without the description, however, he would have known that this was Trebizond.

The man was lean and gaunt, like the carcass of Death itself. His lips were so thin and bloodless that his mouth seemed to be nothing but a straight line drawn in crayon across his face. His eyes were coal-black, and protruded so far that they seemed about to leap out and strike at one. He was standing in such a way that most of his cadaverous body was protected by the chair. He had one of Sue's ears gripped between two of his bony, bloodless fingers. In his other hand a handle to which was affixed a razor blade. He was holding the blade idly in the air above Sue's head.

"Good afternoon, Mr. Klaw," he said. "Let us do away with all pretense. I know that you are Stephen Klaw, one of those three devils who are called the Suicide Squad. And you know that I am Franz Trebizond. I am the one for whom you have been searching. You have found me only because I wanted you to find me. I expected that you would come here to investigate, when I learned that Lisa Monterey had phoned this number from the Groton Hotel. You see, I did not underestimate you."

"Thank you," said Stephen Klaw, bowing graciously. He still had his hands in his pockets.

"You see," Trebizond went on smoothly, "I have been using the home of my good friend, Judge Hinchley, who was once such a violent enemy of the Skull and Swastika. I enjoy converting my enemies into friends—and servants. The Führer gave us an example when he converted France into a servant of his purposes. Just so, I have done with Judge Hinchley... and others."

Judge Hinchley stirred in his seat. "Damn you!" he grated in a hoarse voice. "Damn you for the devil himself!"

Trebizond laughed. "You see, Mr. Klaw, how my friends love me? Judge Hinchley will do whatever I ask of him—because his nineteen year old son volunteered to fight in Loyalist Spain, and escaped to France after the collapse of the Spanish Republican Army. The boy was interned. But when the armies of our glorious Führer conquered France, young Hinchley became our prisoner. Now, the good judge must serve us well, for we have his son as our hostage."

"I see," said Stephen Klaw. His eyes were on the razor blade Trebizond held in one hand, and on the pink ear of Sue Watson which he held with the other. "And now you expect to convert me into the same kind of 'friend!'"

"Exactly. First, let me warn you that at the least suspicious move you make, my bodyguard on the balcony will let fire with four guns, and turn your body into a sieve. For instance, if you should attempt to draw those two automatics you are holding in your pockets, my guards would shoot before you could draw."

A twisted smile tugged at Steve's lips. "Thank you for the warning. Let's hear what you have to say."

"What I have to say is easily understood. This girl—Sue Watson—is a very beautiful and delicate creature, whom it would be a pity to disfigure. I understand you are interested in her. I, too, am interested in her. Because I hated her mother, I should like to dismember her, bit by bit. You see how easily I could slice off her ear. There is so much I could do to her—and enjoy it. Yet I am willing to forego this pleasure—in exchange for a very small favor which you can do for me."

Steve nodded. "I know what you want—the list of the Executive Council of the Skull and Swastika."

"Exactly. You will give up the list. And you will give up your persecution of the S.S. Corps. You will turn your talents to other endeavors. So long as you do not molest us, Mr. Klaw, Sue Watson will remain unharmed."

Sue's face was white and tense. "No, Steve!" she cried out. "Don't give him the list. I don't care what he does to me!"

Trebizond yanked hard at her ear, so that she gasped and bit her lip with pain.

"I want your answer now, Klaw. Or else you will see this girl die slowly!"

"I haven't got the list with me," Steve said huskily.

"Perhaps one of your partners has it then? Kerrigan or Murdoch? They came along with you, I'm sure. No doubt they are trying to get into the house by a window or a back door. I must tell you that it would be very regrettable if they broke in. My burglar alarm system is not the ordinary kind. It doesn't ring a bell. Instead, it releases a flood of deadly gas which kills the intruder as soon as he puts his head inside the window—"

He was interrupted by a voice from the balcony, directly across from where the four guards stood with the machine-guns.

"My, my!" said the voice. "You certainly are very thorough, Mr. Trebizond! It was a good thing that Steve Klaw unhooked the burglar alarm for us!"

STEVE THREW a quick glance up at the balcony, and grinned. Kerrigan and Murdoch had come out of a doorway up there. They must have climbed in through the window in the waiting room, and made their way up through the house. The guards had certainly seen them come out on the balcony, but must have thought at first that they were members of the household, not dreaming that anyone could enter from the outside.

Kerrigan and Murdoch were standing shoulder to shoulder

up there, guns in hand, and facing those four machine-guns at the opposite side of the room.

"*Shoot! Shoot!*" screamed Trebizond.

But it was Kerrigan and Murdoch who started shooting first. Their four heavy revolvers began to blast in a synchronized, thrumming fandango of death. The slugs from their heavy revolvers smashed at the machine-gunners before those killers could recover sufficiently from their surprise to raise their sights from Stephen Klaw on the floor below. The bodies of those gunmen were smashed back against the wall.

And at the same time, Stephen Klaw began to fire his two automatics from his pockets, through the cloth. His left-hand gun lanced three shots quickly at the bald-headed Belding, who had been standing over to one side. With his right-hand gun he fired up at the balcony, to help Kerrigan and Murdoch. He dared not shoot at Trebizond, who, ducking down behind Sue Watson's chair, had drawn a gun.

Klaw leaped forward, across the vast floor toward the chair where Sue sat handcuffed, and behind which Trebizond had taken refuge. He had his automatics out now, but held his fire. He raced forward, hoping to reach Trebizond before the spy-master could harm Sue.

But Trebizond had forgotten about the girl. Snarling with rage, he thrust out his revolver.

Steve saw the muzzle, but kept on coming in at a run. The gun rose, the black hole of the muzzle staring him in the face. In another fraction of a second Trebizond would fire, at almost pointblank range, into Klaw's face…. And then, a hurtling body

201

threw itself headlong into the line of fire just as Trebizond's gun exploded!

It was Judge Hinchley!

The Judge had leaped out of his chair with a hoarse cry, and virtually flung himself upon the bullet earmarked for Steve!

Hinchley fell, the blood gushing from a wound in his chest. And in that instant Stephen Klaw leaped over the desk and sprang around behind the chair. Trebizond uttered a squeal of fright, and raised his revolver.

Stephen Klaw's gray eyes flickered for a moment, and his lips were tight and grim. He thrust his automatic out at arm's length into Trebizond's face, and pulled the trigger.

The blasting of gunfire was echoing and re-echoing from every nook and cranny of the great old house. Kerrigan and Murdoch leaped down from the balcony to join Steve Klaw on the main floor. Klaw went swiftly through the pockets of the dead Trebizond and found the keys to the handcuffs which bound Sue's wrists to the chair. He freed her, and raised her to her feet.

The Judge was dying fast. But that look of utter hopelessness which Klaw had seen in his eyes before was no longer there. And his lips were smiling. Klaw bent low over him, thinking as he did so of that moment last night when he had bent low over a dying woman. She had given up her life, too.

"I've… paid my… debt. Not ashamed… any more! My son— they'll kill him now…."

Stephen Klaw clasped the old man's hand tightly. "I'm sure your son would rather have it this way, Judge."

"Yes… yes. Thank God I had… the courage…." A gush of blood filled the old man's throat, and he died.

Stephen Klaw got to his feet, and put an arm around the shoulders of Sue Watson, who was sobbing quietly. He looked over at the grim, bleak faces of Kerrigan and Murdoch. The three of them were thinking of the same thing—of the hard days ahead, when they would have to round up all the hundreds of members of the Skull and Swastika—many of them honest Americans like Judge Hinchley, who had come against their will, under the thumb of the merciless organization. They were thinking of the heartbreak and the sorrow that would come to many American homes where a son or a daughter or a father had been led into disloyalty by the vile tenets of the S.S. Corps. But they were also thinking that the heartbreak and the sorrow would be a small price to pay to keep America free!